KYLE

SINS OF THE FATHER
EVIL DEAD MC – SECOND
GENERATION
BOOK SIX

By

Nicole James

KYLE

SINS OF THE FATHER

EVIL DEAD MC

SECOND GENERATION SERIES

Book Six

By

Nicole James

CHAPTER ONE

Kyle—

My tires crunch across the gravel parking lot of the Evil Dead MC clubhouse. It's an old red-brick warehouse buried in the back of an industrial park on the wrong side of San Jose. No one ever comes here who doesn't belong.

I back my motorcycle in among my club brother's bikes, drop the kickstand, and swing my leg over.

Marcus, TJ, and Billy stand outside, smoking.

I dig a pack of smokes out of my cut and dip my head to light up. Sucking in a lungful, I feel the tingle as the nicotine floods through my bloodstream.

"Where's Rafe?" Billy asks.

I shrug. "Keeping track of my brother isn't my job."

TJ huffs a laugh. "Since when? You've been like his watchdog for the past couple years."

"Not lately," I snap.

"Heard that chick moved in with him," TJ muses. "How's that goin'?"

"I wouldn't know," I mutter. "The last thing I want to do is get involved in my brother's love life." Especially since I've become obsessed with his girl.

We met her at the same time, but Rafe beat me to the punch. Like I always do, I let him win, not even bothering to give him any competition. It wasn't that I didn't want Sutton. I did. And the way she'd looked at me, I think she was interested. But Rafe swooped in, and I didn't want to get in his way.

"Who the fuck's that?" Billy mutters beside me, drawing my attention toward a silver Mercedes turning in the lot.

"Why does that car look familiar?" I say under my breath.

It comes to a stop on the other side of our line of bikes. The window slides down and a cool blonde who looks in her mid-forties stares at us.

"She's probably lost," TJ mutters, lifting a chin at me. "Find out what she wants."

I toss my smoke and amble toward the car, then dip my head and give her a grin. "Can I help you, darlin'? You lost?"

Her eyes hit the club emblem over the door. "No. This is the place. I need to speak with your president. Is he here?"

Her reply throws me, and I glance at TJ. "She wants your ol' man."

He grinds his cigarette under his boot and opens the clubhouse door a foot, sticking his head inside.

Billy joins me at the car. "What's the problem?"

While he's talking to her, I wander to the back of the car and check the plates. NTGUILTY.

Shit. I immediately realize why this car looks familiar. I gesture to the plate, and Billy strolls over, his eyes following. We exchange a look.

"The club's attorney?" he whispers.

I lift my chin toward the driver's seat. "Must be his widow."

"What the fuck's she doing here?" Billy asks.

Cole pushes out the door and stops in his tracks when he spots the car. Then he approaches, his hands going to the doorframe of the open window as he leans down.

"Joselyn. I heard about Harry. I'm sorry for your loss. He was a good attorney."

"They killed him, Cole," she replies, pushing her shades up to reveal brown eyes and fake lashes.

Cole's chin pulls to the side. "Who did?"

"That's what I need you to find out."

Our prez lifts a brow. "That's a job for the police, honey."

"You and I both know Harry was dirty. The cops don't give a damn who killed him. You're the only one who can help me. Please."

Cole straightens and crosses his arms. "Okay, so I find out who did it, then what?"

She opens her purse wide enough for all of us to see stacks of banded cash. "Then you kill them for me."

Cole grabs the door handle and swings it open, looking a little pissed she's flashing cash and propositioning him for murder in the open parking lot. "Goddamn it, Jos. You can't make an offer like you're ordering a trash pickup."

"I'm sorry. I don't know how this is done." She starts to cry.

Cole sighs. "Come inside. Let's talk in my office."

She climbs from the car, and Prez takes her by the arm, escorting her through the door of the clubhouse.

Billy and I both stare after them, and TJ whistles.

"Who'd have thought Harry Silver would have such a knockout wife?"

"How'd he die?" I ask. "I mean, I heard about it when it happened, but not the details."

"It was in the news. They found him shot in the head, his body dumped in the Edmund G Brown Aqueduct, somewhere out by Santa Nella, I think."

"Was your father close with him?" I ask.

"I don't know."

Green walks up, hearing the end of our conversation. "Harry was a slick asshole, but he won, and that's all we cared about. Plus, he was dirty as hell—always giving Cole the down-low on any rats on probation we needed to track down."

Red Dog joins us, and Green grins at him.

"Remember that little weasel drug dealer who kept movin' into our turf? The one in them apartments near Fruitvale and Piccoli Road?"

Dog laughs. "Yeah, I remember. You tried to jump up to the second-floor walkway like you were an acrobat. Fell and almost broke your back."

"Why you gotta be like that?" Green's shoulders slump.

"Like what?"

"I'm tryin' to tell a story here. Tryin' to educate these boys, and you gotta bring up my failings. It's very hurtful."

Dog rolls his eyes. "But Green, your failings are always the best part of the stories you tell."

"Fuck you, Dog."

"Bite me," he replies, then looks at us. "Come on, youngins. Soon as Cole finishes with the lady, we're having Church."

We follow him inside and go to the bar. I take a seat at the end with a clear shot of the room. I'm on my second beer, my thumbnail scraping the label, thinking of the day Rafe and I took Brayden and Rebel out to Santa Cruz.

"Hey, space cadet." TJ waves his hand in front of my face. "Look who just walked in."

I turn to see the woman I'm obsessed with coming through the door with my brother, Rafe.

"Great." I return to my beer.

TJ laughs, probably because he knows my fake nonchalance won't last thirty seconds. And he's right. I can't help my eyes from roving over her.

Sutton has that surfer girl look—sun-kissed skin, ocean blue eyes, and sandy blonde curls. We met her on the wharf at Santa Cruz last year. It wasn't until a week ago that I heard she'd moved to town to be with Rafe.

The two of them wander toward the pool tables. Sutton scans the clubhouse until she finds me. Then she smiles, before Rafe tugs on her arm and they disappear toward the back.

TJ's gaze follows them, then he twists to study my face. "I don't understand why you let Rafe move in on her. I heard from Brayden she was into you that day you all met. She coulda been yours, Kyle."

"Rafe wanted her. End of story." I tilt my beer up.

"But so did you. What rule says you always gotta let him win?"

"She's with my brother. I'm happy for him."

"Live life for yourself and no one else, Kyle." TJ offers advice I don't want to hear. "His happiness is not your responsibility."

"Just drop it," I growl.

"You can't keep making everything easy for Rafe. What happened that night at Gigi's shop was not your fault."

"Enough," I snap, and several heads turn my way. Last thing I want to do is relive the night I almost lost my brother.

CHAPTER TWO

Kyle—

It's not long before Harry Silver's widow leaves, and Cole emits a sharp whistle.

"Church, boys. Now."

We all follow down the hall and into the room, gathering around the scarred wooden table with the Evil Dead emblem carved into it—three skulls that look like they're screaming.

Cole sits at the head, and the officers take chairs around the table. Crash, our VP, Red Dog, Billy's father, Green, Shane, Jake, Cajun, Reckless, and my father, Wolf. The rest of us stand along the side.

I cross my arms and lean against the wood paneling.

Once Cole dispenses with the formalities of roll call, he gets down to the business at hand.

"We've got two charity runs before Sturgis, boys."

It's mid-March, and Sturgis is five months away. I don't know why he's already bringing it up, but I don't really care. He talks with some of the officers about making plans.

I'm wondering if he's going to say anything about the chick in the Mercedes, when he gets quiet, rubbing his palms back and forth and staring at the table.

"I've, uh…*we've* been approached about something. Most of you never met him, but Harry Silver was our club's attorney. Had been for years. I first met him back in the day when Mack ran this chapter." He looks around the room, and the corner of his mouth pulls up. "Some of you were too young to remember much from those days. Anyway, Joselyn thinks he was murdered. Wants us to find out who killed her husband." He drags a hand down his jaw, stroking his beard. "Not a lot to go on. She filled me in on what she could."

"And what's that?" Wolf asks.

Cole motions to Crash. "You want to give 'em the details, VP?"

Crash leans forward, his gaze traveling around the room. "He was found in the aqueducts north of Santa Nella."

Green frowns. "Santa Nella? That's across the Diablo Range, ain't it?"

"Out where Christ lost his shoes," Red Dog mutters.

"Actually, there are a lot of almond growers out there. The place is covered with orchards," Crash explains. "His widow thinks he had taken on a case of one of them—a grower by the name of Machado. Claimed his orchards were being contaminated. Thought it was coming from a nearby construction company. She said he talked about some gravel pit where he thought chemicals were being dumped."

"That all we've got to go on?" my father asks.

"No, Wolf. She said he'd found out about some airstrip out there. He was following leads, and it took him out to Las Vegas the week before he died. Before he left, he told her he'd figured it all out, and he was going to stop those sons-of-bitches."

When Crash stops talking, I glance around the room.

Shane leans in his chair. "So, we're gonna become private detectives now or some shit?"

"I'm doing it as a favor to a grieving widow. That, and I'd like to know what the hell's going on in our own fucking backyard," Cole bites out.

"That's just it, prez. It's seventy miles away. That's hardly our backyard," Green says.

"Close enough," Cole snaps with a lifted brow.

Crash grins. "Plus the lady's payin' us."

That gets everyone's attention, and men lean forward.

"How much?" Jake asks.

"Two-hundred grand," Cole replies.

Reckless whistles. "We split it equal?"

Cole nods. "Fourteen and some change each."

"I'm in," Green says, grinning.

Cole puts his elbows on the table. "We'll need to do some research. I really want to go over a map of that area where they found him, and that almond grower, and construction company. Plus, I'd like to locate that airstrip. She's going to bring by his case files later."

"That Las Vegas trip worries me," Reckless muses. "I mean, I know they say there's no mob in Vegas anymore, but there's a ton of money, and men who deal with tons of money do whatever they have to do to protect it."

"Agreed. We're gonna take our time with this. I don't want to drag the club into the middle of something that can get us killed." Cole looks around the table. "Officers, we'll get into it more tomorrow." He slams the gavel down. "Meeting adjourned."

We walk out, and I grab another beer at the bar. The ol' ladies are playing pool, and I like seeing they've taken Sutton into their group, welcoming her like I knew they would. This club has a great bunch of ol' ladies, and it's growing every day.

Resuming my perch on my barstool, I see my brother approach the pool table and sling his arm around Sutton, leaning to give her a peck on the lips.

Billy, TJ, and Marcus follow me to the bar.

"We're all taking a ride down to Joey's. You comin'?" Billy asks.

I shake my head, noticing Sutton and the rest of the women slipping on their leather jackets. "Nah. Think I'll stay here."

TJ puts an arm around my neck and pulls me off my stool in a headlock. "Wrong answer, grasshopper. You're goin'."

They drag me to my motorcycle, and everyone mounts up. Strapping on my helmet, I watch Rafe throw his leg over his bike. Sutton looks hot as hell in a tight leather jacket that fits her like a glove. She gets on behind him and wraps her arms around my brother. He reaches back to pat her thigh, and I turn away, my jaw tightening.

I'm going to have to watch her and my brother all night. Fucking hell. Tapping the heel of my boot to my kickstand, I slip on my shades, already planning to cut out early.

CHAPTER THREE

Sutton—

Riding in a pack is like nothing I've ever experienced, especially when it's with a club like the Evil Dead. They ride in tight formation, weaving in and out of traffic and changing lanes like a fine-tuned machine. It's something I'm sure only extremely skilled riders can manage.

It feels formidable. Thrilling. I don't even know how to describe it, except that I love it.

I find Kyle in the row behind us. His head moves slightly in my direction when he catches me looking. His eyes are hidden behind his shades, and the sinking sun reflects off them. He looks so badass on his bike, commanding it easily.

The first time I laid eyes on him, I was attracted to him, but it was his brother who hit on me. Kyle had heat in his eyes when he smiled, but he backed off the moment Rafe made a move.

It's been there between us ever since—this unspoken, unrealized attraction. I know he feels it. Sometimes I catch him looking at me, and I see it in his eyes. Even the way he tries to avoid me tells me there's more behind those looks than he ever lets on.

I wish I felt free to break it off with his brother, but every time my eyes fall on his scar, I can't bring myself to do it.

Perhaps that's why Kyle defers to Rafe in all things. Perhaps he feels sorry for him.

It's not that Rafe isn't a great guy. He is. It's not that he isn't attractive or fun to be with. I just don't have that connection with him.

I thought maybe if I moved here to be with him, things would progress, and I'd get those feelings. But I'm not sure it's ever going to happen. I know Rafe has fun with me, and we get on well, but I don't know if he's interested in anything permanent.

I've been a free spirit for years, but I know in my heart I'm ready to settle down.

I have to be sure I'm doing it with the right man.

The bikes slow and make a left turn into the parking lot of a nightclub that already looks packed. A marque out front proclaims its bike night, and the place is slammed full of motorcycles, chrome gleaming in the fading evening twilight and the neon of the club.

Loud music pours from inside, and people mingle in and out of the doors and onto the outside patio. The club finds an area, and they all back in one by one, like a well-choreographed dance.

When Rafe's bike comes to a stop, I climb off and unbuckle my helmet, while he drops the kickstand and kills the engine. All around me, other couples do the same. Billy and Melissa, Marcus and Brandy, TJ and Gigi, Harley Jean and Reckless, with Green and Kyle the only two loners. The rest of the older club members hung back tonight.

I've never been to this bar, but it looks like a lot of fun.

Rafe takes my hand, and we fall in with the others, making our way to the door.

It's wall-to-wall people, and I stay close to Rafe as we wind through the crowd.

We end up at a table outside in a rear courtyard. I get the vibe that Kyle would like to sit as far away from me as possible, but by the time he and Green bring up the rear of our group, the last two seats left are directly diagonal to me at the end of the table and across from me.

Green grabs the seat across from me, leaving Kyle next to me, and he doesn't look too happy about it. Spinning his chair around, he rests his forearms on the back.

We chat for forever, it seems, and we still haven't seen a waitress. Rafe, TJ, and Billy go up to the bar to get us a few pitchers of beer. While they're gone, I can't help letting my gaze drop to take in the bulging muscles and the tattoos covering Kyle's arms. The work is good. Really good. He looks like a total badass.

His eyes catch and hold mine for a moment before he breaks contact and says something to Green about the plug wires on his bike.

I sit awkwardly until Harley slides into Rafe's empty seat. "How's it going, Sutton?"

"Good. How are you?"

"Want to go throw some darts?" she asks, nodding to the electronic dart boards inside the door.

"Sure." We step inside and grab an open machine.

Before I throw the first dart, Harley steps over to me.

"So what's the deal with you and Kyle?"

I frown, panicking on the inside, wondering if my interest has been plain on my face. "What do you mean?"

"You two barely speak. Does he not like you dating his brother or something?"

I shrug. "Not that I know of. I guess you'll have to ask him."

From the expression on her face, she doesn't like my answer. "Before Brayden and Rebel left for Alabama, she told me she thought there was a real connection between you two before Rafe stepped in and made a move. Is that true?"

My gaze goes over her shoulder and out the big windows to the patio, finding Kyle. He's looking my way. By now Rafe has returned to the table, and he's talking to Kyle, who points over Rafe's shoulder toward us. Rafe twists and spots us, then rises from his chair.

I don't have much time.

"Harley, if you want the truth, it was Kyle I was interested in when we first met, but he never made a move. Or maybe Rafe just beat him to it. After that, he pretty much looked away and got quiet."

She studies me for a moment. "You know why, don't you?"

I shake my head.

"Because of the shooting. Didn't Rafe tell you how he got that scar on his forehead?"

"Not really. He said there was a problem that had to do with the club. I got the feeling he didn't want to talk about it."

"I don't think he even remembers what happened."

I frown. "What?"

She checks over her shoulder, Rafe moving quickly toward us.

"Meet me tomorrow at the diner across from Gigi's tattoo shop," she murmurs low, then turns a bright smile on Rafe. "Want to join our game?"

He gives her a big grin and wraps an arm around my waist, pulling me against his side to press a quick kiss to my lips. "Why don't you girls have a beer before the pitcher gets warm?"

I glance at Harley Jean, and she answers for both of us.

"Sure, Rafe. No problem."

I think she just doesn't want to insist on us playing. I wonder if it bothers her that he's interrupted. If so, she isn't saying so. Respect for the MC? Or maybe she doesn't want to rock the boat between him and I."

I want to say something, but I go along. I'm new to this world and not sure how close they keep tabs on their women. Is he being protective or controlling? Or am I reading too much into this? Perhaps, like he says, he just wants us to enjoy the beer while it's still cold. He did go to the trouble of standing in line to get it for us.

We return to the table, and Kyle's eyes flick between Harley and me, and I can't help thinking he's wondering what we were talking about.

Rafe pours me a glass and passes it with a grin.

We sit and drink until all the pitchers are empty, and I'm having a great time. These guys are a hoot, and the laughs just keep coming.

Billy pours the last of the final pitcher into his glass and leans forward, like he's sharing a secret with the table. "You should have seen Green the other day. He dropped a twenty-dollar bill on the street in front of Gigi's place."

"Did he try to chase it?" Kyle asks, giving Green a look that says he knows he did.

"What're you lookin' at me like that for?" Green lifts a brow.

"Because I know you, bro," Kyle replies.

"Of course, I chased it. It was twenty damn dollars." Green splays his hands.

Billy chuckles. "He chased it half a block. Every time he'd get close, the wind would blow it another ten feet. I tried to get a video of it on my phone, but I was laughing too hard."

Kyle leans toward Rafe and sniffs. "You wearin' cologne, brother?"

"Maybe," Rafe replies, looking embarrassed. "What's it to ya?"

"It's nice. Kind of a leather and mesquite sort of deal." Kyle grins. "Like a barbequed baseball glove."

Billy almost spits his beer out.

I tilt my head. "You guys always like this?"

"That's just brothers busting each other's chops," Green says. "Don't pay it no mind."

"Right," Rafe says. "It's comradery. Like Batman and Robin."

"Right. I'm Batman. He's Robin." Kyle jerks his thumb at his brother.

Rafe lifts a brow. "Who're you callin' Robin, asshole? I'm Batman."

"Come on, Dynamic Duo." Green polishes off his beer and

stands. "Let's hit the road."

We all stand to leave, and when we get out to the bikes, Rafe looks over at his brother.

"Hey, Kyle. Follow us to my place. I need your help with a delivery I got today."

Kyle tugs his gloves on, slowing the motion. His eyes dart to me, then back to his brother. "What do you need me for?"

"Just follow us back, okay?"

TJ and Billy stare at Kyle, as if they're listening to see what he'll say. They swing their legs over their bikes, but adjust in their seat, not firing their engines up.

"Yeah, sure. Whatever you need, brother," Kyle replies.

TJ shakes his head, looking pissed, then fires his bike up.

Rafe seems oblivious. I climb on the bike behind him, and Kyle follows us to Rafe's place.

Rafe rents a cute but small Craftsman house he told me was built in 1925. It has a lot of character with a big bay window, but it's showing its age.

As for the neighborhood, Rafe told me it's on the edge of the Little Portugal North neighborhood. The Portuguese catholic parish is two blocks over, and we hear the bells chime three times a day. I think they annoy Rafe, but I find them to be soothing.

Kyle pulls into the driveway behind us and follows us up the stairs of the front porch.

There's a flyer on the front door.

"What's that?" I ask.

Rafe nabs it and smiles. "It's the church bulletin. Mrs. Vargas lives next door. She works for the church. She's always trying to get me to attend. Guess she thinks my soul needs saving, and she seems determined to see to it. Last summer, she and her husband invited me to the Feast of the Holy Ghost. It was pretty cool. They're a sweet old couple."

He unlocks the door, and we enter into a long living room that continues through to the back of the house. Tall wainscoting comes up the walls, and the floors are the original hardwood. There's a pretty set of corner windows with seat benches underneath and leaded glass on the top of the windows. It's charming. I've sat curled up in that window, reading. It's my favorite thing to do.

The main bedroom is in the front of the house on the left. It's the room that has those pretty bay windows visible from the street. Again, there's leaded glass on the top transom of the window that flood the room with light.

While the house has tons of charm, it also needs tons of work.

Rafe leads us out back. There's a garage with a small apartment in the rear. There is no grass to speak of... just blacktop.

Rafe has set up a small seating area with cheap lawn furniture around a movable firepit. The space had potential, but this wasn't it.

There's a big cardboard box leaned against the garage. It's about three feet wide, a foot deep, and six feet tall.

"What's that?" I ask.

"I ordered a gazebo."

"Tell me you didn't call me all the way over here to set that thing up tonight," Kyle says.

"No. I just need help moving the box. The tenant in the apartment can't get the garage door up with this in the way." Rafe's fists land on his hips. "Besides, you live all of three minutes away, asshole."

I turn to Kyle. "I didn't know you were so close."

"About a mile west of here," he replies.

"So, like walking distance?"

His brows lift. "Not for you. You get near my house, the neighborhood is okay, but there's a good bit of industrial area you'd have to cross to get there. It wouldn't be a good idea for a single woman to walk that route."

"Well, my girl's not walking to your house, bro. So, it's irrelevant." Rafe throws his arms around my shoulders.

"I'm just sayin'." Kyle looks at the box. "Let's get this damn thing moved, if we're movin' it."

They go to lift it, and Rafe gives Kyle the heavy bottom side.

"Fucking hell, Rafe. What's this thing made of?"

"Wrought iron."

"You couldn't buy an aluminum one, motherfucker?" Kyle strains to lift it and shoves the big, unwieldy box around the corner.

His biceps bulge with the effort, drawing my eyes.

"Aluminum ones are crap," Rafe snaps.

They set it down, and Kyle straightens. "That it? Or you want me to come in and fix your plumbing, too?"

"Shut up, wiseass."

"You're welcome, dickhead."

I elbow Rafe. "Say thank you."

"Thanks, bro. I appreciate it."

Kyle huffs a laugh. "You owe me one. Or maybe it's more accurate to say, you owe me fifty."

"Ha ha."

Kyle heads down the drive.

I look at Rafe. "You could be nicer to him, you know. Sounds like he does a lot of favors for you."

"Guess he does. You gonna be on my case, too, like Mrs. Alvarez? You tryin' to save my soul, baby girl?" He walks backward, following his brother.

"That's up to you, Rafe. Some things you have to do for yourself."

CHAPTER FOUR

Kyle—

Rafe catches up to me at my bike.

"Hey, man. Wait up. I wanted to talk to you about something else."

Apprehension fills me, wondering what he wants now. I drag in a slow breath and exhale, then turn to face him. "What's that?"

"It's about Sutton."

My gaze strays to the house. "What about her?"

"She needs a job. I wanted to ask if you could give her one."

"Me?" Just the thought of being with her for hours every day sends terror through me. How in the hell would I stand it?

"Now that you've got that food truck, you're your own boss, so you could hire her. Besides, you're always sayin' it's hard to keep a good employee."

"Rafe, I don't know. I'm just getting the business off the ground. Money's tight, and it's not like I can pay her much." My brain scrambles for any excuse I can think of, but even to my ears, it sounds like I'm clutching at straws.

"I think she's just looking for something to occupy her day. Being new to town, she's spending a lot of time sitting around the place, waiting for me to get back."

"Why the hell would she want to do this kind of work?"

"She told me she has fast food and restaurant experience. She'd be perfect for you."

"And what happens if she screws up, and I have to fire her? How awkward is that going to be?" Terror settles into my gut.

"You won't have to fire her, Kyle. She'll be a great worker."

"And how would you know?"

"I feel it in my bones."

"Great. I should hire all my employees based on whether or not my brother gets a feeling in his bones."

"Quit being a wiseass. If she doesn't work out, she doesn't work out. No hard feelings. Just help me out here."

"I'm helpin' you out a lot lately."

"Come on, Kyle."

"She know you're out here askin' me this?"

He glances toward the house. "No, man. I mean, I didn't say I was going to ask you tonight. I just figured, why wait?"

"So, what does that mean? Does she want to work on a food truck?"

"Probably."

"Probably?" I huff. "You haven't asked her about this, have you?"

He wobbles his head. "Not exactly. When she told me she'd worked in the food service industry before, I figured it'd be perfect."

I give a heavy sigh and throw my leg over my bike. "I'll think about it. That's the best I can give you right now."

He nods. "That's all I'm asking."

"You don't ask for much, do ya?" With that, I fire up my bike and pull out, heading home. Jesus Christ. Has he lost his mind? There's no way I can work with Sutton day in and day out. Maybe I won't have to give him an answer. Maybe when Rafe fills her in, she'll blow her top and tell him off. Right now, I think my best plan of action is to ignore it and avoid Rafe for the next few days, until this ridiculous scheme of his sputters out.

I make a couple turns and hit East San Antonio Street, heading west, and finally I pull into my own drive, dog-tired and dragging as I go up the steps of the front porch.

I live in a small house a lot like Rafe's, but it's in a nicer neighborhood with tree-lined sidewalks, and this place was built in the 1930s.

My place has a red brick patio in front and a massive stone chimney climbing the wall. Walking in the door, the living room is on the right, the big fireplace taking up a good portion of the front wall. Like Rafe's place, I've got the original hardwood floors. The living room leads to a dining room with French doors that open to a flagstone patio and built-in planter boxes. My place may not have the architectural details and charm of my brother's, but the outdoor space makes up for it. The lush landscaping makes for a peaceful oasis—one I use often to unwind for the club.

I grab a beer from the fridge and sit at the glass table on the deck and listen to the crickets. Leaning back, I can't see a lot of stars, what with the populated area, but there's a pretty crescent moon hanging on the horizon.

I think about my brother. We'd been inseparable growing up. We did everything together, even prospected the club together. When you saw one, you saw the other. Until that fateful day at Gigi's tattoo shop. He went out to check the alley, and I let him go alone. I can still hear the gunfire. Crushing guilt has followed me every moment of every day since I ran out and found him on the ground, blood pouring from his head. Every day since, I've felt a huge responsibility for my brother settle on my shoulders. I've routinely sacrificed my own dreams, needs, and wants for the sake of making life easier for Rafe.

He won't admit it, but he's been different since that day. His personality has shifted a bit, and he doesn't seem as sure of himself. Even my parents won't admit anything is wrong. But I know. He's not the same guy.

I also know what I've been doing. I'm self-aware enough to see it. I've been feeling sorry for Rafe, afraid to 'leave' him, afraid to push him to do the things he used to do. Rafe was the most confident, self-assured guy I knew—at least in my age bracket. He never second guessed a single decision. Now, he's afraid to *make* a decision.

That's why the whole thing with Sutton has been so shocking. I'm surprised he asked her to move in. It was a big step. Huge. And he made it with no more thought than a snap of his fingers. At the time, I thought maybe he knew a good thing when he saw it.

But he doesn't seem as connected to her as I thought. It's like he's holding her at a distance, like she's a passing fling. And I hate it.

I wonder if she's, in a way, doing the same thing I have: afraid to leave him. Perhaps she's staying with Rafe, even though he's not the right man for her.

Fucking stop thinking about it, Kyle.

I down my beer and stroll into my bedroom, stopping at the dresser and pulling my club rings off to drop them in the silver tray where I keep them. I sling my leather cut off and hang it over the chair in the corner. Stripping down, I drop into bed, exhaustion heavy on my bones. Stacking my hands under my head, I stare at the ceiling, my mind filled with images of Sutton.

She looked real pretty in the courtyard patio at Joey's. That place has been around since the eighties and has become a legendary drinking establishment. I think it makes most of its money on bike night.

I had to really struggle to keep my eyes off her with her blonde curls gleaming in the moonlight. All I wanted to do was sink my hands into those soft tresses and carry them to my nose, inhaling their fragrance. Would they smell like coconut shampoo? Or maybe something more exotic?

Closing my eyes, I grit my teeth and remind myself for the

hundredth time she's my brother's girl. I try to block the images of her from my mind, but it's no use. My brain won't shut off.

Images of the two of us in the food truck, working side by side, fill my head. It's cramped quarters, with no way to escape each other. We'd have to work together well, or it'd be a living hell. Fuck, why am I tormenting myself with these thoughts?

Jesus Christ, shut up about it. You cannot even think of hiring this girl. It would be a disaster of monumental proportions. The temptation to cross the line with her would be ever-present, and I can't do that. She's the one girl I absolutely cannot have. No one fucks around and steals their brother's girl.

It's bad enough he's my biological brother, but he's also my MC brother, and that shit for sure is not done in the club.

So, why do I keep thinking about it?

I roll to my side and punch my pillow. There's no way she can work for me. I have to make sure that's clear.

CHAPTER FIVE

Kyle—

My alarm goes off, and I crack an eye open, find my phone on the nightstand, and turn it off. And all at once the shit with Rafe floods back.

Fuck.

There's no way I can hire his girlfriend.

How the hell can I get out of this without admitting the real reason?

In all the long hours I lay awake last night, I didn't come up with anything better than avoiding my brother.

I pull on a pair of sweatpants and pad into the kitchen, lighting a smoke and making a cup of coffee. Stepping onto my back porch, I sit at the small table and check out the view. It's almost noon, and I haven't had a single message. Maybe that's a sign it'll be a good day.

I text TJ.

ME: WHAT'S GOING ON TODAY WITH THE CLUB?
TJ: YOU, ME AND BILLY ARE GOING WITH COLE TO SILVER'S OFFICE. CHECK THROUGH HIS FILES FOR ANY INFORMATION WE CAN USE TO FIGURE OUT WHO PUT TWO BULLETS THROUGH THE BACK OF HIS HEAD.

ME: GREAT. WHEN DO WE LEAVE?
TJ: MEET AT HIS OFFICE IN AN HOUR.
ME: WHERE THE HELL IS IT?
TJ: DOWNTOWN. 28 N 1st St

By the time I pull up at the designated address and back my bike to the curb, I'm five minutes late. The other three beat me here. Cole, Billy, and TJ stand on the sidewalk.

"You're late," Cole snaps.

"Sorry. I took a wrong turn, ended up on a maze of one-way streets." I step on the curb and lean back to stare at the ten-story structure. It's an older building judging by the art deco style of architecture. I'm guessing maybe 1930s. "This the place?"

"Yeah." Cole remains on the sidewalk, smoking a cigarette.

"We goin' in?" I ask.

"Waiting on the widow to let us inside," Billy replies.

We stand around a few minutes until the silver Mercedes whooshes down the street and parks at the curb. The pretty blonde climbs out of the driver's seat and approaches. My eyes sweep down her. She's dressed in slim jeans, heels, a light-colored trench coat, and a designer handbag over her arm. She hardly looks the part of a grieving widow, but what would I know about it?

"Cole, thank you for coming." She puts her hands on his arms, then looks at the rest of us. "I thought you'd be alone."

Our prez may be in his fifties, but like Brad Pitt, he's aged well.

"This is some of my crew, Jos." He nudges her hands off him. "Show us Harry's office."

She leads the way into the building, past the guy at the desk who stands and practically trips over himself to bow to her.

"Mrs. Silver. I heard about Harry. I'm so sorry."

She nods, but doesn't stop as she leads us to the elevator.

He eyes our leather cuts and Evil Dead patches. "Is everything all right, Mrs. Silver?"

"Yes, Chad. Thank you." She hits the button; the doors glide open, and we all step on.

It's small and crowded with all of us. I stand to her side and inhale her expensive perfume in the tight space. She pushes her designer sunglasses on her head. It's only then I notice the red rims around her eyes. She hides her grief well, but it seems she really is torn up about her husband's death.

We exit on the third floor and follow her down the hall. She stops at the end in front of a set of double doors. A brass plate reads, LAW OFFICES OF HARRY SILVER, SUITE 310. She inserts a key and lets us inside. We step into a reception area with a desk on the right and a couple of chairs set up like a waiting area.

Cole lifts his chin to the desk. "Who sits here?"

"That would be me."

Cole cocks his head. "You worked together?"

"Is that so hard to believe?" She doesn't wait for a reply. "Harry's office is through here."

Straight in front of us is an open doorway that leads to a small room. A soft drink machine takes up a good portion of it. She walks through, and we follow, all of us stopping dead when we see a massive safe the size of a small refrigerator sitting just on the other side of the wall. It looks like it's been here since the building was built.

Cole points to it. "You keep a lot of cash in this?"

"He did." She lifts a brow. "I gave you most of it yesterday."

Cole's jaw tightens, and she leads the way into the next room.

It's a large, deep office. A huge bookcase takes up the left wall, and surprisingly, the place is decorated with a lot of personal stuff. There are the standard framed licenses and diplomas behind the desk, but there's also a variety of odd things that show another side of our lawyer. There's a framed Joe Namath football jersey on the wall, a samurai sword next to it, an autographed photo of Keanu Reeves, a golden buddha, and a free-standing gumball machine, of all things.

Harry Silver was an odd man. Or maybe he was an onion with many layers.

Joselyn moves behind the desk, unlocks a file drawer and takes out a stack of three file folders, plopping them on the desk. "These are the cases Harry was working on when he died. Nothing of much importance."

"What were they?" Cole asks.

She lifts the first one. "Tyler Mann. Beat up his wife in a drunken rage. First offense. I'm sure Harry was going to get him off on probation. He'd have no reason to kill my husband." She lifts the next file. "Joey Garza, three-time loser with a penchant for car theft. He was in lockup at the time of Harry's murder."

"And the last one?" Cole asks.

"The almond grower I told you about. The one in the San Joaquin Valley who came to Harry for help, trying to get the person responsible for dumping chemicals in the creek upstream from his orchards." She checks the name on the file folder. "His name is Machado. Mateo Machado."

Cole folds his arms. "I didn't know Harry did that type of law."

"Environmental? He didn't. But, regardless of what you think of him, Harry had a heart. He felt sorry for the guy. He's a third-generation grower just trying to hang on to the family farm." She lifts her chin. "You think there might be something there?"

"I don't know. Maybe whoever polluted the stream is a heavy hitter. You mess with the wrong people, they get pissed." Cole makes a motion with his hand, indicating he wants to see the file.

"It seems like a stupid thing to kill a man over." She passes it to him.

Prez plops in the leather chair in front of the desk and flips through the file.

I study the bookcase and all the law books and odd bookends and knickknacks, thinking about how I never really knew the guy.

Cole holds the folder up. "Can I take this?"

"Of course. Do you really think that's the key?"

"I don't know. You said there was no money missing, and he wasn't killed here, so I'm thinking whoever did it lured him out for a meeting. Unless there was a new client you don't know about, I'm thinking we start with this guy." He studies her. "Anything else you can think of?"

"No." She pauses. "Just the trip to Las Vegas the week before he died."

"And you think it's connected to this case? You said as much at the club."

"Yes, but he never told me all the details."

Cole lifts a brow. "I'm guessing his murder had nothing to do with the wife-beater or the car thief. Sounds like it was either this case or a new client. He didn't tell you more? Seems odd. You worked with him."

"I was busy that week. Our daughter is getting married." She looks forlornly to the floor. "And now she'll have no one to walk her down the aisle."

Cole frowns, and we all shift on our feet.

"I'm sorry about Harry, Jos. I'll do what I can. Can you get his phone records from the company you use?"

She nods. "Of course."

"It'd be helpful if you mark which numbers you recognize and who they belong to."

"I'll do it today."

"The day he went missing... What happened?"

"We were both in the office. I was consumed with wedding plans. There was a meeting with the caterer that afternoon. When I left the office, he was still here, working at his desk."

"So, I'm thinking he got a call that lured him away."

She searches our prez's eyes. "I'll get the phone records."

Cole holds up the file. "We'll talk to Mr. Machado."

She steps closer to Cole and takes his hand. "I really appreciate your help. I don't know what I'd do without you, Cole."

"I can't promise anything, Jos."

"I understand."

Prez pulls his hand free. "Call me when you get the phone records."

We head out the door, and she stays behind.

Cole looks back. "Lock the door after us."

She frowns. "You think I'm in danger?"

"Until we figure this out, it's best to be cautious. Whoever did this might come here looking for something. We just don't know."

"I'll be careful."

We head to the elevator and ride down. Walking out, Chad the doorman gives us a wide-eyed stare.

"Where's Mrs. Silver?" he asks, like we just left her upstairs with her throat slit.

"Relax, Chad," Cole says. "She had some calls to make." He approaches the man and rests his fists on the desk.

Chad leans back in terror.

"Did you have any unusual visitors the week Mr. Silver died?"

Chad shakes his head. "No. No one. I swear."

We leave the man shaking in his shoes and walk to our bikes.

"What do you think?" TJ asks his father.

"I'm thinking we drive to Machado Almond Co." He flips open the file and checks the information. Then pulls it up on his phone's map app. "Looks like the orchard is near the intersection of I5 and I40, north of Santa Nella. Come on. Let's go, boys."

"How far is it?" Billy asks. "I've got a little over a half a tank."

"Eighty-nine miles. You'll make it. There's a gas station at the exit."

We mount up and head out.

CHAPTER SIX

Kyle—

An hour and a half later, we pull off the exit and stop at the gas station. My phone goes off, and I pull it out of my hip pocket, glancing at the screen.

Rafe.

Grinding my teeth, I shove it back where it was.

TJ notices. "Who was that?"

"My brother."

TJ chuckles. "Probably calling for your help again."

"Oh, he's already waiting for an answer from the last thing he asked me to do."

"Yeah? What's that?"

"He wants me to hire Sutton to work for me."

"On the food truck? What'd you tell him?"

"I gave him a bunch of reasons why it would be a lousy idea. He kept shooting them down. So, I told him I'd think about it. My plan is to avoid him until he forgets about it."

"And how's that workin'?"

"Well, I'm out of town, so so-far so-good."

"Holy shit."

We turn and stare at our president, who's looking at his phone.

"What's the matter?" TJ asks.

"Check this out, guys." Cole faces his phone toward us. "I pulled up the area on my map app. You can see the neon green crap polluting the stream in the satellite image."

"Whoa," I say. "I wonder how toxic it is."

Billy glances at the horizon. "Where is this place?"

"We head east. First road, we take a right and head south."

Five minutes later, we roll up a driveway and stop in front of a white clapboard farmhouse with a big porch.

A thin, gray-haired man with skin browned from the sun comes out with a shotgun leveled at us. "Who the hell are you?"

Cole holds his hands up. "We're here on behalf of Harry Silver's widow. She asked us to look into his death. You Machado?"

The barrel of the gun lowers. "I had nothing to do with that."

"I'm not saying you did. He was working a case for you, wasn't he? I just want to know about that. Can we talk?"

A girl opens the door. We don't get more than a glimpse, but she's a looker. "You okay, Daddy?"

"I'm fine. Go back inside."

Machado sets the gun against the railing. "Have a seat."

We join him on the porch.

Cole extends his hand. "Cole Austin."

"Mateo Machado." He and Cole shake hands and take the two rockers.

"Sorry about the greeting. You can't be too careful, and you looked like trouble."

"We can be, if we need to be. Guess that's why Joselyn asked me to help."

"That his wife's name? He never said, though I remember he told me their oldest was getting married. I'm sorry for their loss. Heard about it on the news. Some detectives came by last week asking questions."

"You know anything about his death?"

"No. Like I told them, I had nothing to do with it."

Cole nods. "Tell me about what he was doing for you."

"He was helping me get some compensation for the contaminated creek killing my orchard."

"Isn't that a matter for the EPA?"

He rolls his eyes. "Yeah, try calling them. You'll get nowhere."

"So, what was Harry going to do for you?"

"He was going to find out who was dumping chemicals into the creek." He points to the west. "Just upriver."

"Show us."

He stands. "We can take my pickup."

The two of them climb in the front, and the three of us crowd into the crew-cab. He pulls onto the road.

It's an older truck, and Cole rests his arm in the open window, watching the orchard of almond trees flash past us.

"There much money in the almond business?" he asks.

"It's a decent living. We aren't as big as some places around here, but it's all I know. My grandfather started this place in the forties. There wasn't much out here back then."

We drive for a bit, and he makes a couple of turns so we come up along the opposite side of his property. He pulls to the side of the road just before a small bridge over the creek. We climb out and approach it. Standing high on the bridge, we get a good look at all the neon green muck that was visible from the satellite map image. It's got a nasty smell as well.

"Gross," TJ says.

"Exactly," Machado agrees.

Cole scans the west side, pointing to a gravel section. "They're coming down off the road right there and dumping it."

"Yep."

"Have you tried to catch them?"

"I've set up game cameras, but I get nothing on camera. Just end up with my units taken."

"How often do they come?"

"There's no pattern."

"When was the last one?"

"About a month ago."

"And it still looks like this?"

He nods. "I've found some wildlife dead around here, too."

Cole lifts his chin. "Looks like a dead fox down there."

"It's such a shame."

We return to his truck.

"Anything else you want to show me?" Cole asks.

"There is."

Machado drives us to the other side near his house and slows at the far end of his property, coming to a stop but not getting out.

He points to the side of the road near a small dirt trail entrance. "See the sign warning people to keep out? My neighbor put it up."

It's hard to miss. The thing is the size of a shipping pallet and is mounted between two posts.

Cole reads it aloud. "*Keep out. No trespassing. Absolutely no more riding. Not a public place. This is private property. No trespassing. Sheriff will be called and vehicles impounded.*" He turns to pin Machado with his eyes. "Dude sounds pretty serious. What's that about?"

"We've had problems with dirt bikers. The creek runs between our properties. I don't care if the kids want to ride there. It doesn't bother me as long as they stay out of my groves, which they do, because what the hell do they care about some almond trees?"

"Seems like a lot of trouble when they're doing no harm." Cole spots a camera on a pole and points to it. It's aimed at the road from the entrance to the trail, which has a new-looking chain-link fence.

"That's a lot of security." Cole lifts his chin. "What's over there?"

Machado shrugs. "I don't know. Gravel pit is what I thought it was. Trucks come and go."

Cole pulls it up on his satellite map again. "This the place?"

Machado looks over his shoulder. "Yeah."

"You know what this is?" Cole points to something. "Looks like an airstrip."

"Yeah. Sometimes a plane lands over there. Mr. Big Shot flies around in a private plane, I guess."

"Mr. Big Shot?"

Machado shrugs. "Property is in the name of Warren Drake. I only know that from looking up the docs online. Never met the guy."

"How often do these planes come and go?"

"Every couple of days. Usually just before sunrise, I'll hear one come in. It never stays long."

Cole frowns. "Have they got landing strip lights over there?"

Machado shrugs.

"They come this morning?"

"Nah."

"So maybe they'll come tomorrow?"

"Probably."

"Mind if we go across your land and check out what's going on over there?"

"You think it's why Mr. Silver was killed?"

"Maybe. Security cameras, mysterious pre-dawn flights in and out... Something's going on. Maybe Silver stumbled upon it when he was trying to find out who polluted your stream."

"So, if I hadn't contacted him for help, he'd still be alive?" The man looks forlorn.

Cole slaps a hand on his shoulder. "I'm gonna find out who killed him. It wasn't you. You didn't want anyone dead, so don't feel guilty."

He nods, but I'm not sure he's buying Cole's words. "Still, I got this ball rolling."

"Let's go check it out."

Machado returns us to his property.

"You got a pair of binoculars?" Cole asks.

"Yeah, give me a minute." He disappears inside and returns with two of them. Then he leads us through the orchard of trees toward the back of his property.

"Stay away from the left side of the grove. The bee keepers are busy today," Machado warns.

I give a side-eye to the nearby trees, hearing the buzzing among the pretty white blossoms. The ground is covered with white petals.

"Look at all these," Billy says, kicking some up with his boot.

"They call it valley snow," Machado says. "Lasts from February to mid-March while the almond trees are in blossom." We come out at the far end of the rows of trees, and he points at the creek and a dusty dirt hill rising on the other side that runs the length of his property. "That's where they used to dirt bike. You'll see the trails."

Cole stares at the creek. "We need to get across."

Machado points to the left. "It's pretty shallow down that way."

We head downstream and find a place to avoid getting our boots soaked.

"There may be more cameras," Cole says. "Stay low. You two go that way." He points to Billy and TJ, passing them one set of binoculars, then looks at me. "You're with me, kid."

We get low and move up the hill until we can see over it. There's a maze of dirt bike trails and some old plywood jumps they've made with boulders. We lie flat on our bellies, and Cole looks through the binoculars.

"See anything?" I ask.

"There's an airstrip and a metal shed. Looks like an old gravel pit, but nobody's working it."

"You see any vehicles?"

"Nope. Not a soul."

We stare at each other.

"So, they've got all this security," I muse. "But no one's out here."

"Maybe they only care about it when that plane comes in."

"What are you thinking?" I ask.

"I'm thinking they're smuggling drugs and distributing them by hiding the shipments under the gravel they haul out. Who's gonna dig through it if they get pulled over?"

"So, you think Harry stumbled across this?"

"I think Harry contacted the owner. Since he's not on the property, maybe he found his contact information listed with the county property records. He sent them a letter. Maybe he even met with this guy. He probably just wanted some basic information since his property borders on the other side of the contaminated creek. Maybe he was thinking a class action lawsuit against the EPA or something. Who knows?"

"If this guy's doing illegal shit, that wouldn't make him too happy," I add.

"Exactly. I'm thinking Harry knew nothing of what was going on in the middle of the night, but the last thing this guy wants is a government agency snooping around."

"So, he had Harry taken out?"

Cole shrugs. "It's just a theory, but it makes sense."

"And Harry's trip to Vegas?"

"Maybe that leads to Warren Drake, the guy listed on the deed."

"Now what?"

Cole studies the land. "I'm gonna leave TJ and Billy out here tonight. See if they get lucky."

"Then?"

"Then hopefully we'll know what we're dealing with."

"If a plane flies in, you want them to follow the truck when it leaves?"

He shakes his head. "I'm not getting my guys killed over this, but I want to know what's happening in our own fucking backyard."

"Maybe we take a load," I suggest with a grin. "Steal the product out from under them."

"It may come to that. I just want to know how big a fish we're dealing with first."

The four of us head into Santa Nella and grab some lunch at a diner. Over cheeseburgers, Cole tells TJ and Billy everything we discussed.

"Man, I never expected this when we headed out here," TJ says, dragging a fry through a puddle of ketchup.

Cole pulls up the map app on his phone.

"You realize that almond farm is seventeen minutes from where they found Harry Silver's body?"

"Really?"

"Yep. Just a little over seven miles."

"They didn't go far, did they?"

"Why should they? I'm sure they figured they'd never get caught."

"From Machado Almonds to Las Vegas is 470 miles, seven hours via I5 and I15. If they take the back roads, it's 508 miles and a little over nine hours."

"Maybe they're going closer," I suggest.

Cole checks his app. "It's about 280 miles to Los Angeles, about four hours and forty-five minutes. Just under a hundred miles to San Jose, about an hour and a half drive. San Francisco is about the same."

"Lots of places they could be headed," Crash mutters. "My guess is LA."

"We'll see," Cole replies.

"What the hell are we supposed to do out here until midnight?"

Billy asks.

"It's almost three now. You really want to haul ass to San Jose just to turn around in a couple of hours and ride back?" Cole replies.

"Guess not."

"Machado said you can wait at his place until nightfall. Maybe his daughter will bake you a pie or something," Cole teases with a wink and a kissy face.

"If there's nothing I need to do with the club, I can work tonight, but I'll need to get going soon, so I can have the food truck ready for the dinner crowd," I say.

Cole nods and picks up the check. "Let's hit the road."

We leave TJ and Billy at the diner and head to San Jose.

CHAPTER SEVEN

Kyle—

I'm busy as hell trying to keep up with the line at the food truck, when my brother sticks his smiling face in the window.

"Bro, what's cookin'?" He's so fucking funny.

"Hey, Rafe. What are you doing here?" My eyes go over his head to where Sutton stands behind him. She's wearing a tank top with a sweater over it, and a pair of shorts and Uggs. Her blonde curls are in pigtail knots on top of her head. She looks adorable, in a college coed sort of way. I force myself to drag my eyes away.

Rafe peers in. "Looks like you're working all alone. I can help you out with that." He loops his arm around Sutton and tugs her forward. "Give her a chance, man. She's a hard worker."

I huff a laugh. How would he know if she's a hard worker?

"Hey, mister. Where's my order? I've been waiting twenty minutes," a customer complains.

"I'll have it right out." I sigh and turn to Rafe. "Okay. Fine. She can help me tonight, and we'll see how it goes."

"Fantastic. You won't regret it, Kyle."

I'm regretting it already, but I meet them at the rear door, just in time to witness my brother kissing her goodbye. "I'll be back to pick you up. Just call."

I hold out my hand and help her into the truck, then toss an apron at her chest. "You ever cook?"

"Um, sure. I cook."

I give her a look. "Know how to chop stuff?"

"Sure."

I hear my brother's bike roar away. I'm now alone with his girlfriend. Well, except for the half-dozen people waiting in line for food.

Sutton ties on her apron. "So, what do you make?"

"The specialty is chicken chili tonight, but it's not ready yet. I was late setting up. Right now, they're ordering tacos."

"Oh." She sounds less than enthused.

"What does *oh* mean?" I shove a paper tray at her. "Two beef. One chicken. All soft shell."

She shrugs and begins filling the order. "Nothing."

"Tell me." I work side by side with her, filling the next order.

"It's just… every truck in town sells tacos."

"And I need something more original, right?" I pass the orders out the window.

"Maybe."

At the end of the line, I go back to tending the chili. "That's what this is for. It was our mother's recipe." I grab some curry and twist the cap off, about to shake it into the pot.

"Wait. What is that?" She puts a hand on my arm.

"What is what?" I reply.

"What are you about to add?"

"Curry powder."

She makes a face. "What would you add that for?"

"It's my mother's recipe."

"You sure about that?"

I grab the recipe I have under a magnet on the stainless hood and hand it to her. It's in my mother's handwriting. "Says so right here."

She scans it. "I don't see curry on here."

"Right there." I point.

"That's cumin. That's an m, not two r's."

I grab it out of her hand and squint at the cursive. "You sure?"

"Pretty sure. I guess you could call and ask her."

I do just that. "Ma? It's Kyle. What's this ingredient in your recipe? I thought it said curry, but Sutton says it's cumin." I study her. She's standing before me with her arms crossed, so sure of herself. "Okay. Thanks."

I disconnect, and Sutton throws me a big grin.

"I was right, wasn't I?"

"Yeah."

"Good thing I saved the chili. No one would have liked it with curry."

"You don't know that."

She grunts out a laugh. "Oh, I'm pretty sure."

"Quit rubbing it in. You were right. Thank you for saving my chili and my ass."

"You're welcome." Her grin grows. "Hey, look. We're having an actual conversation."

"We've had conversations," I defend.

"You've barely spoken two words to me since I came to town. What gives?"

A customer walks up, and I wait on him, thankful for the distraction.

Of course, she doesn't let me off the hook, and starts up as soon as we're making the order.

"Did I offend you, Kyle?" Her voice is soft.

"Nope," I reply, not looking up from what I'm doing. I don't want to see her concerned expression, and I don't want to get sucked under by sad, puppy-dog eyes.

"Am I not good enough for your brother? Is that it?"

I sigh. "I don't think that."

The chicken chili is ready, and we dish up three servings along with my mother's cornbread recipe, and pass them to the man and his companions.

"Well, what is it?" she asks.

"You don't let up, do you?"

"Nope."

"This is exactly why this isn't going to work. This is why I told Rafe this was a mistake."

"You told him this was a mistake? He told me you were looking for help. If not, then why did you agree to it?"

I fling a hand toward the window. "Because he showed up and pushed it on me."

"You mean pushed *me* on you." She unties her apron. "If you want me gone, I'll go."

"Look, I tried to avoid him for exactly this reason."

"What reason?"

"Because we've got no business spending hours on end together. Especially in these tight quarters where we can't escape each other."

"You need to escape from me?"

I stop and slap the rag on the counter. "Don't play dumb. You know why."

"Maybe you need to learn to say no to your brother. I've noticed you never seem to do that."

"I can say no to Rafe."

She crosses her arms. "Really? When's the last time?"

"Just get back to work."

"Maybe this arrangement might help the two of you. Ever think of that?"

"Help us? How?"

"You'll have to learn to deal with him."

"I deal with him just fine."

"And he needs to learn to stop asking things of you. He needs to learn to stop using you as a crutch."

"A crutch? Is that what I am? You've been here, what? A month? And you've got it all figured out," I snap, irritation in my voice.

"I didn't say I had all the answers, but I know what I see. He leans on you more than he should. Surely, you can agree with that."

I hate that she's right. I also hate that she's pretending not to know what the real problem is. Or maybe she's pretending it doesn't exist. Or *maybe* it's because she doesn't feel any vibe happening between us. For some reason, that pisses me off even more.

"Whatever. Can we work and not talk?"

At that moment, the man I served the three orders of chicken chili approaches the window.

"Hey, man."

I dip my head. "Yes, sir?"

"I wanted to let you know how much we loved this stuff." He holds up his bowl. "This chili is awesome." He gestures to the bench where the two women he came with are sitting. "My girlfriend went on your social media and left you your first five-star review." He gives me a thumbs up. "I just wanted you to know."

"I appreciate it. And tell her thanks so much for the review."

"She's going to tag Food Truck Tina in a post and rave about it. Maybe she'll come and try it. A good word from her can do amazing things for your business."

"Really? Who's Food Truck Tina?"

"She's a food critic in the Bay Area. Every season she gives a top ten list, and if you earn one of her Five Forks Awards, your business will go through the roof. It happened to a friend of mine in San Francisco." He scrolls on his phone and turns the screen toward me. "This is her social."

Sutton leans out the window and snaps a photo of his screen.

"Thanks, mister. We'll be sure to check her out. We'd love for her to come try our chili."

"Have a great day." He wanders away.

I stare at Sutton. "You ever hear of this person?"

Her face lights up with excitement as she scrolls through her phone. "Oh, my God, Kyle. She's big time. A good review from her is like magic. She can literally make or break a business."

"What if she hates it? If she posts a bad review, my business is over before it gets off the ground," I grumble.

"What if she likes it? What if she says your food is fantastic? It could mean everything. You've got to be positive."

"I'm positive," I argue.

She huffs. "You are totally a glass-half-empty kind of guy."

I want to defend myself, but… maybe I am. I never used to be. When the hell did that happen?

I pick up the spatula and start scraping the grill with jerky motions. Great. Now I'm the sad-sap Eeyore character who thinks everything is doom and gloom. That's not exactly the way I want Sutton to see me, but apparently, she does.

Fucking fantastic.

CHAPTER EIGHT

Kyle—

Two days later, I've got the Food Truck up and running for the dinner rush, and Sutton is supposed to be here helping me, but she's twenty minutes late.

I wonder if she's decided not to show at all. Great. I fought having her here, and now I realize I've already come to depend on her.

Pulling out my phone, I shoot her a text.

ME: WHERE ARE YOU?

SUTTON: I'M COMING.

ME: YOU MUST BE THINKING OF ME THEN

SUTTON: HA HA.

ME: WELL HURRY YOUR ASS UP

SUTTON: I'LL BE THERE IN A MINUTE. AND DON'T PUT THAT DISGUSTING SPICE IN THE CHICKEN CHILI BY MISTAKE

ME: YOU'RE NOT THE BOSS OF ME. I'LL DO WHAT I WANT

SUTTON: THEN YOU'LL RUIN IT AND DRIVE ALL YOUR CUSTOMERS AWAY. THEY MAY EVEN TURN YOUR TRUCK OVER IN PROTEST

ME: YOU'RE HILARIOUS. IF ONLY YOUR COOKING WAS AS GOOD AS YOUR JOKES

SUTTON: ARE YOU CALLING ME A BAD EMPLOYEE. OH, IT'S ON.

ME: NO, IT'S NOT.

SUTTON: OH, IT'S ON LIKE DONKEY KONG

ME: YOU'RE A WEIRDO. I'VE GOT TO GO. I HAVE CUSTOMERS WHO LOVE MY CHICKEN CHILI. THERE'S A LINE.

SUTTON: THANKS TO ME

ME: TRUE

I grin, tuck my phone away, and get to work. The smile stays on my face. It's hard to be in a bad mood around Sutton, even with the stress of keeping up with the line or when something goes wrong behind the grill.

She shows up five minutes after our text exchange, and we work side-by-side, but not too close. I keep my distance because the smell of her is driving me wild. At one point, she takes a picture of the line and then taps away on her phone.

"What are you doing? Get back to work, slacker."

"I'm posting the picture of the line and telling everyone to come on down for some delicious chicken chili."

"Oh. Why would you want to post there's a line they'll have to wait in?"

"It's called social proof. It tells them that if others like it, so will they."

"So, now you're my marketing expert?"

"Yep. I need a raise."

"We haven't broken even yet."

Her shoulders wilt. "We haven't?"

"You think all this is cheap? It costs money." I start ticking a list off on my fingers. "There's the loan I'm paying on the truck. Permits.

Parking fees. Insurance. Food. Fuel."

"Okay, okay. I guess I'll have to post more often. I've got to come up with something that goes viral. Maybe you could do a handstand. Oh, can you do a backflip? Maybe shirtless?"

I roll my eyes and point with my tongs. "Get back to work."

I may sound tough, but I grin when she turns away.

The sound of motorcycles carries to us and echoes off the metal trailer. They roll to a stop and shut off their engines. A minute later, TJ, Marcus, and Billy appear.

TJ's eyes cut to Sutton, and he lifts his brows at me. I know what he's thinking. *What the fuck's she doing here?*

There's only one person waiting for food.

"You got this, Sutton? I need to talk to the guys."

"No problem."

I open the back door and hop down. Tonight, I'm parked near a courtyard off a busy street down the block from a popular farmer's market. My brothers take a seat at one of the picnic tables provided.

"What are you doing here? Come to have some dinner?"

TJ's eyes go over my shoulder to the trailer. "I see you caved. I heard it was true, but I had to witness it with my own eyes. What happened?"

"Rafe dumped her on me the other day. I didn't have much choice."

"So, how's it going?"

"We had a bit of a rocky start, but it's going surprisingly well."

"Glad to hear it."

"How'd it go the other night?" I ask, my voice low. TJ's answer is equally soft spoken.

"A plane came in; we watched them unload what looked like some bricks of heroine. A dump truck loaded with gravel showed up, and a guy jumped out with a shovel, and they buried the packs."

"No shit." My brows lift.

"The truck pulled out, and the plane took off. The entire transaction took under ten minutes."

"Wow."

"Yeah," Billy adds. "They were a well-oiled machine."

"I wonder how long this has been going on," I muse. "Rafe said he and our dad were going up with Cole and Crash tonight."

"Yeah, they're going to stake it out. If they show again, they're going to follow the truck this time. See where it goes."

"Did the dump truck have any chase vehicles for protection?"

Marcus leans his elbows on the table. "They had two guys in a pickup truck. Cole said if they can't get close to the dump truck, they'll try to see if they can get lucky and put a tracking device on one of the vehicles."

"How they gonna pull that off?" Fear for my brother fills me.

Marcus shrugs. "Hopefully, they'll stop for gas or something. Maybe they can catch them at a truck stop."

"Maybe I should go with Rafe." I'm already thinking about pulling my phone out and calling him.

TJ cocks his head. "You're not his personal bodyguard, Kyle."

"I know that." My face flushes.

"Rafe can take care of himself."

"Can he?" I snap, and TJ tightens his jaw.

"Besides, bro," Billy cuts in, "your father will be there. Wolf will watch his back. You know that."

"Guess so." My gaze flicks to Sutton, visible through the window. "Where do you think they're hauling this stuff?"

"Could be anywhere," TJ replies.

Billy shrugs. "My dad thinks LA, but Prez isn't so sure. He thinks that trip Silver made to Vegas has got to be connected, seeing as it happened right before he was murdered."

"I wonder if he knew what he was getting wrapped up in," I murmur.

"Probably figured something out. Maybe he talked to the wrong people, and it got him killed."

"Yeah. I just don't want it to get any of us killed," I say. A line is starting to form at the truck again.

"Looks like business is good," Marcus observes.

"Yeah. Sutton's been helping me out with posts. She's really good at it. It's been getting us a decent crowd of followers. Business increases every day."

"That's great," TJ says.

"I've got to get to work, guys." I stand.

"Sure. No problem." Billy stands as well.

"You want some food?" I offer.

"Nah, we've got to get going," TJ says, rising himself.

They head to their bikes, but TJ pauses.

"Oh, by the way. Your dad volunteered you to cook for the clubhouse picnic on Saturday."

My shoulders slump. "Seriously?"

TJ grins and swings his leg over his bike. I climb in the trailer and move next to Sutton, and begin filling orders. We work silently, and it feels good to be next to her.

She catches me staring. "What?"

"You doing anything Saturday?"

CHAPTER NINE

Sutton—

Saturday, when Rafe and I ride up to the clubhouse, there's already a crowd. I see Kyle's food truck parked in the lot. Kids run around the picnic tables.

Kyle is busy filling orders.

Rafe parks his bike, and we climb off. The place is packed, lines of bikes and people I know don't all belong to the club crowding the limited space. I see guys with other patches and a lot of riders with no patches at all.

"I didn't realize there'd be so many people," I say.

Rafe takes my helmet and hangs it off his handlebar. "Yeah, a lot of hang-arounds and friends of the club get invited. It's kind of an open party we have every spring."

"Kyle wanted me to help him."

"Make sure he pays you," Rafe teases with a smile, then pulls me to him for a kiss. "I'll steal you away for a break in a bit."

"All right." I head over, Kyle's eyes following me through the crowd. When I climb in the back door, he turns.

"Hey. Thanks for helping today."

"No problem. What do you need me to do?"

"I'm making tacos, burgers, and brats. If you could make sure we have enough chopped onions and sliced tomatoes, that'd be great."

"Sure."

He's got an air fryer going with some onion rings.

"Those smell terrific," I say. "Are they frozen ones?"

"Fuck no. I came up with the recipe myself. Here, try one." He passes a ring proudly and slides me a cup of dip. "Gotta try it with my secret sauce."

I dip and bite into the crispy batter coating. The onion ring practically melts in my mouth, and the sauce is amazing. "Oh, my God. Why haven't you been making these all along?"

"I've been fooling around with the recipe. I wanted to make sure I got it perfected."

"These are definitely a hit. These are going on social media immediately."

He grins. "So, I can cook, huh?"

"Guess so. You just can't read your mom's handwriting," I tease.

"Right." He laughs and throws more burgers on the grill.

We work for a couple of hours with barely a break in the line. Finally, we get a few minutes with no one at the window.

"Wow. That was crazy," I say.

"Yeah, this crowd can eat." He busies himself by wiping down the counter.

I stare at him until he turns and catches my eyes. "What?"

"Can I ask you something?"

He slows his rag. "Sure."

"Why do you let Rafe take advantage of you?"

"Is that what I do?" His rag moves faster.

"Yeah."

He shrugs. "He's my brother."

"He's capable of doing things on his own, you know."

"I suppose he is." He pauses and studies me. "And how's Rafe treating *you*?"

"Fine. Why?"

"You think he's using me. I want to make sure he's not using *you*."

I sober at his words. Maybe I deserved that for sticking my nose in something that isn't my business. "Touché."

"I'm not trying to be a dick, Sutton."

"Well, mission failed." I turn and start chopping an onion vigorously. I feel Kyle watching me.

"You tryin' to kill that onion?"

"Since I have a knife in my hand, I guess you're lucky it's only an onion I'm attacking."

"Hey."

"What?" I ask, without looking at him.

"Sutton?"

"What?" I say again.

"Put the knife down."

I do and finally look at him.

"You didn't answer my question. How are things between you and my brother?"

"It's none of your business, Kyle."

He drags in a breath. "Maybe not, but I'd want to know if he wasn't treating you right."

I cross my arms. "And what would you do about it?"

"Beat the shit out of him," he says without hesitation.

I read the truth in the depths of his eyes. "Would you?"

"Absolutely."

"I appreciate your concern, but he and I…"

"What?"

"We're fine. Everything's fine."

"Why doesn't it sound like it?" He growls, like he's at the end of his patience.

Green walks up to the window. "Hey, Kyle. Fill me up a plate, will ya?"

"Sure, man." Kyle goes about it, and while he does, I pitch in, grabbing some onion rings hot out of the fryer, then passing Kyle a container of dipping sauce.

"You two work good together," Green says, taking the plate from Kyle. "Thanks, man."

After he walks off, I busy myself chopping onions. Green's right—Kyle and I do work well together, and I look forward to seeing him every day. I realize I'm happier on the days I know I'm going to be spending it with Kyle. It's a feeling I know I don't have with Rafe. He's fun, and we have a good time, but it's like there's no depth to our relationship. I don't think we've had a single conversation about anything serious.

"Sorry I snapped at you." Kyle leans a hip against the counter.

"You want to know what I think?" I ask.

"Of course. I mean… I know I can be gruff, and I've given you a hard time, but you're a good worker, and your views, opinions, and feelings matter to me."

My mouth drops open. I stand there for a second before I blink and gather myself to reply.

"That may be the nicest thing anyone's ever said to me," I whisper.

"God, I hope not," he replies and wipes his hands on a rag.

When I don't reply, he tilts his head, studying me.

"My brother doesn't say things like that? He doesn't tell you you're important to him?"

My eyes start to glaze, and I pick up the knife.

"You okay?"

"I think the onion's getting to me." I wipe my face with my apron hem.

Kyle lays a hand on my shoulder. "Sutton—" Someone approaches the window, and he turns. "Hey, Rafe. You hungry?"

My eyes widen. Did he see us? Did he see his brother's hand on my shoulder? But when I brave a glance, Rafe's grinning.

"Just came to steal Sutton away for a break." He looks past Kyle to me. "You ready, babe?"

My gaze shifts to Kyle. "If it's okay with you."

"Sure. I've got this."

I untie my apron, and Rafe meets me at the back door, threading our fingers together and leading me toward the clubhouse. I dare a peek over my shoulder and find Kyle watching.

Rafe leads me inside and gets me a beer. Then we wander over to a poker game, and he asks if he can join in. I hang in a chair next to him, bored.

After twenty minutes, I lean to Rafe. "I need to get back and help Kyle. He's manning the truck alone, and there are a lot of people here."

Rafe barely glances at me, reaching for his glass. "Yeah, sure. I'll walk you out."

"That's not necessary. Finish your poker game." I stand, and he grabs my hand, bringing it to his mouth for a kiss, then tugs me down and kisses my mouth.

"I'll come by in a bit."

"Okay." I make my way through the crowded clubhouse. When I climb in the back of the truck, there's a line, and Kyle is rushing around. "Sorry, I should have stayed."

His gaze flicks to me for just a split second. "Can you get another batch of tacos ready? I need six more. I've got burgers going, but I need to get another batch of onion rings in the fryer." He's busy chopping onions.

"On it." I get to work.

With the grill going, the trailer is hot, even though it's a cool day. Kyle's wearing an Evil Dead t-shirt with the sleeves torn off, and his tanned, inked biceps glisten. He looks hot as hell... in the sexy meaning of the term.

We work until the line is gone and finally have a minute to breathe.

Kyle tosses a spatula and leans against the counter. He grabs a bottle of water and chugs it all, his throat working and droplets trailing down. When he lowers the bottle, our eyes connect.

"Where's Rafe?" he asks.

"Playing poker."

Kyle nods and looks away. Now that we've got a moment and I can observe him, I notice something's bothering him.

"What's wrong?"

He huffs a laugh. "I suppose you'll think it's hilarious."

"What's that?"

"Melissa and Harley Jean signed me up on a dating app."

"You're kidding?" I grin.

"Nope." Sliding his phone from his back pocket, he pulls up the app and turns the screen to face me.

"Did you know about this?" I scan the text and photo.

"Not until just a while ago. They came by and dropped the bomb on me." He returns his phone to his pocket.

I giggle. "They did it as a joke, right? Did you tell them to take it down?"

He doesn't answer immediately, just crosses his arms and stares at his boots. He huffs a laugh. "It's too late for that. They already set a date."

I straighten, and something like panic flashes through me. "Oh. I see. Are you going?"

"Kind of have to. I'm supposed to meet this girl at a restaurant tomorrow night."

I feel like all the air sucks out of the trailer. "Did they…" I pause and swallow. "Did they show you a picture of her?"

He digs his phone out again, scrolls, and turns the screen toward me.

My eyes shift to his face. "She's beautiful."

"Yeah." But he doesn't sound excited.

"Does she know you're in the club?"

He laughs. "I doubt it."

"Are you going to tell her?"

He shrugs. "I don't know."

I suddenly have this forlorn feeling, like I'm losing my best friend. "I, um, wow. Well, good luck, I guess." I sound like a bumbling moron.

"You ever been on a blind date?" he asks.

"No."

"Me neither."

"You're a very good-looking man. Surely, you're not nervous about it."

"Nah. Just not sure how this is done."

"I'm sure it will be fine." Our eyes lock.

"I guess."

"Which restaurant?"

"Sully's on Second and Main."

"Oh."

Someone comes to the window, and Kyle steps over to take their order. It's Sara, Green's ol' lady. She has a little girl on her hip.

"Hey, Kyle. I was wondering if you had any apple juice or something for the kids."

He holds up his finger. "Give me one second."

He moves to the small freezer and appears with a popsicle. He peels it open, revealing the cherry red ice pop.

"Here you go, honey," he says, holding it out for the little girl. "Cherry's your favorite, right?"

She nods, grinning.

"See? I remembered from last time." He reaches out to ruffle her curls. "She's adorable, Sara."

"Thanks, Kyle." Sara turns to her daughter. "What do you say, sweetie?"

"Thank you," she whispers softly, burying her head in her mother's shoulder.

I study Kyle's face. It's lit with a big grin as he watches them walk away. He's leaning on his elbows. When he straightens, he catches me staring.

"What?"

I shake my head. "You're good with kids."

He shrugs. "It's not hard to be good with kids, is it?"

"For some it is."

Soon there's another line, and we work until dark, then clean the equipment until Rafe comes and gets me.

"Thanks for the help," Kyle says.

"I'm exhausted." But I'm grinning. "How 'bout you?"

"Yeah. Oh, wait." He reaches for the tip jar and holds it out to me. "Here."

"I can't do that. You have bills to pay."

He rolls his eyes, grabs the cash, and shoves it in my hip pocket. Butterfly tingles shoot up my body at his intimate touch.

"You earned it."

"Thanks." I search his eyes wondering if that touch affected him as well, but he gives nothing away. I step out of the trailer.

Rafe sticks his head in. "Hey, Kyle, can you give me a hand moving this picnic table?"

"He's exhausted, Rafe. Find somebody else," I snap.

"He's standing right there."

"He has to shut everything down. He's worked all day, unlike you, who played poker and enjoyed yourself."

"What's the bug up your ass?" Rafe asks.

"Never mind." I stalk off, and he follows.

"Babe. What's your problem?" He catches up to me as I head to his bike. In my mind, I'm wondering if we get in a fight in the middle of the clubhouse parking lot, if I can find my own ride. Of course, I still only have his place to go to. It's times like this that I miss my girlfriends. I've met the other girls here, but it's not the same.

Rafe catches my hand and spins me around. "Hey, I'm sorry."

"You always do this, Rafe." I sigh.

"Do what?"

"Ask Kyle to help you with shit. Why? You're not helpless. Learn to do things for yourself. Or if you need help, you have a dozen MC brothers you can ask. Why is it always Kyle?"

"He's my brother."

"That doesn't mean he always has to drop what he's doing to come help you."

"What the hell has gotten into you?"

I jerk my hand free. "Nothing. I'm tired and want to go home." I stalk to his bike, and when I reach it, I cross my arms and stand there.

He doesn't say another word, just passes me my helmet, climbs on, and fires the bike up, then waits while I climb on. As we ride through the lot, I see Kyle watching us pull out.

CHAPTER TEN

Kyle—

We're an hour into the lunch rush, and word of mouth has evidently spread about my chicken chili and cornbread. And my homemade onion rings are a big hit. There's a line ten deep.

I'm glad because I know I can't be open for dinner, thanks to Melissa and Harley setting me up on that damn blind date. I mean, the girl is beautiful, but I've never been great at hitting on women, and making small talk with strangers isn't at the top of my list, either.

Sutton is helping me, and when I look over, she's reaching for her phone.

"Give me a minute, okay?" She heads toward the door.

"Where are you going? We have a line."

"I know. Isn't it awesome? I'm going to grab a couple of pictures and post a video. It'll only take a few minutes."

I roll my eyes. "Hurry."

I keep up with the orders, but also continue to have one eye out the window. Sutton takes a few selfies with the camera over her head, getting the line and food truck in the shot. When next I check on her, she's doing a video, interviewing some people in line.

After about ten minutes, she comes back inside.

"I got some great stuff. They really love your food. Word is starting to spread. I can't wait to get this posted." She's staring at her phone, her fingers moving over the screen.

"Do you have to do that now? I could use your help."

"Just one more second…" Her second takes more like sixty seconds before she finally slips her phone in her pocket.

The line doesn't die down for almost an hour, but I can't complain. We're raking in the dough—at least enough to keep the bills paid this month.

When we get a breather, Sutton slips her phone out and scans it.

"Oh, my God."

"What?" I snap.

"The video I shot? It already has a ton of views. This thing could go viral. Wouldn't that be amazing?"

"Sure, but that's like lightning striking. There's no way to control it."

"I get that, but it's still fun to hope."

Once the lunch rush is over, I start shutting things down.

"What are you doing? We're going to have a crowd tonight. I just know it," Sutton insists.

"I appreciate your enthusiasm, but I've got that date to get to."

"Oh." Her faces falls. "I forgot about that. Sully's right?"

"Yeah."

"But I did all this marketing. People will show up."

"I can't do anything about it."

"Do you want me to run it tonight?"

"Alone? No way."

"Why?"

"It's not safe. I don't want you out here by yourself. What if somebody tried to rob you?"

"You really are a glass half empty guy."

"Looking out for you doesn't mean… You know what? Just forget it."

"Do you not trust me to run it?"

"I'm sure you could. For me, it's the safety issue, that's all."

"Well, I guess it's nice to know you think I'm capable."

"Of course you're capable. Why would you think otherwise?"

She shrugs and won't look at me.

"Sutton, what's wrong?"

"You want the truth?"

"It would be nice, yeah."

"Maybe… maybe I don't like the thought of you going out on this date."

My chin pulls to the side. "Why?"

She shrugs again.

"You're living with Rafe, Sutton."

"I know who I'm living with, Kyle."

"Then I guess you have no business commenting on my dating life."

"I guess I don't."

"But it bothers you?"

"What if she's a nut-bag?

I huff a laugh. She's adorable. "A what?"

"What if she's a crazy lunatic?"

"Why would she be a crazy lunatic?"

"Maybe she's got twenty snakes at home or a tarantula. Ever think about that? What if she eats soap or chews with her mouth open? What if she keeps bees in her backyard? She might even be a hoarder." Her eyes widen. "What if she's a prepper?"

"Did you get too much sun today? Because the only one sounding like a lunatic is you."

"I'm just looking out for you. Isn't that what we do for each other?"

"Sure."

"I'm just sayin', if you need an escape from your date, call me."

I grin. "Hopefully, that won't be necessary."

"Right. But if she's got a bunch of weird piercings and starts talking about UFOs and Big Foot, text me. I'll come rescue you."

"Um, you saw her picture. She doesn't have a bunch of weird piercings."

"Because no one in the dating app world ever posts a picture that looks nothing like them."

"That's sarcasm, right? Because I really don't know what people in the dating app world do."

"Good luck. Have fun. Bye."

"Now you're pissed."

"Nope. Everything's fine. I'll close up. Go enjoy your date."

"I will."

"Good."

"Are we having a fight?"

She throws a wooden spoon at me, and I climb out of the trailer to take down the sandwich board sign and start closing up. Obviously, I'm not leaving Sutton here alone.

I spot her texting and five minutes later, Rafe pulls up to pick her up.

She climbs out of the truck, and we barely speak.

"Bye, Sutton."

"Bye," she throws over her shoulder in a hurry to climb on behind Rafe, who barely lifts his chin at me.

I stand, watching them disappear down the street.

CHAPTER ELEVEN

Kyle—

I pull up near the restaurant and park. Climbing out of my truck, I straighten the cuffs of my black button-down shirt. I've got on a pair of dark wash jeans and a thick silver chain bracelet peeking out of the cuff. I don't do loafers, so I've got biker boots under the jeans.

Hopefully, I'm dressed for this place.

Harley Jean told me it's a fancy steakhouse. I've never been here, but my reservation is for seven. This girl's name is Zora. She's supposed to meet me at the bar.

When I enter, I check in with the hostess, and she says my table should be ready in the next five to ten minutes, so I head to the bar called Sky. It's one of those places that looks turn-of-the-century but modernized. The floor is small black and white tile. A wooden barback takes up the entire wall, but it's all painted dark blue, and the bottles lining the glass shelves in front of the mirrored background are lit in neon. The barstools are sleek, black leather with gold trim. The crowd looks like a mix of men in suits and women in classy workwear.

Zora texted me she'd be in a black strapless top. I spot her immediately. She's at a seat at the bar, a fancy drink in a martini glass sitting in front of her; its yellow color and sugared rim makes me think it might be a Lemon Drop Martini.

She's breathtakingly beautiful—long dark hair down to her waist, piercing hazel eyes, and pale olive-toned skin.

As I approach, I realize she's taking selfies on her phone, and I hang back, waiting to see if she'll finish.

She takes them at every different angle in her seat. It's like watching someone trying out to be a supermodel, and it turns me off.

I step between her stool and the one next to her.

She doesn't notice me the slightest bit.

"Zora?" I finally say.

She breaks her concentration long enough to glance up. "Oh, hey. It's you."

"It is." I extend my hand. "Kyle. Nice to meet you."

The bartender approaches, and I order a drink, standing next to her stool.

Before we can even begin to chat, she lifts her phone and leans toward me to take a selfie of us both. One would be fine, but she tilts her head and makes fish lips, snapping off shot after shot.

Then she takes a video. "Hey, everyone. This is Kyle, the guy I was telling you all about. Isn't he gorgeous?" She turns and addresses me. "They all think you're gorgeous, by the way." Again, her attention turns to the camera. "He's even better in real life than in his pictures."

Hell, I don't know what pictures she's seen.

She squeezes next to me again, turning her body in ways where she can get me into the picture. "Don't we make a cute couple, peeps?"

I find it sort of rude and annoying. It seems like the only thing she cares about is taking selfies and communicating to her friends and followers that she's on a date. Her entire focus is to ensure that everybody in the world of social media knows she's out with me.

She starts talking about the bar and how the restaurant is ultra-chic.

My drink is delivered, and not long after that, they announce our table is ready.

I drag her from her phone long enough to move to the restaurant and follow the hostess to our table.

The place is fancy, with tablecloths and dim lighting.

Immediately, she pulls out the phone again and comments on the restaurant like she's doing a travel guide review of the place.

I don't say much while she drones on, although she gives me the impression she's used to guys lavishing her with constant attention. I'm trying not to cringe, and I'm in utter shock at how addicted she is to her phone. She's more into the idea of creating a fantasy world rather than being in the moment.

The server comes with menus and rattles off the specials, which she barely listens to, but is all too eager to get the man in her shot.

"This is Gary, our server."

Like the entire world cares. I guess some people live vicariously through these posts.

We order wine, and he fills two glasses while my date continues on her phone like I'm not even here.

I have to say something. "Zora, look, I'm not trying to be rude, but the phone has got to go."

She blinks, uncomprehendingly.

"Can you put it down, please?"

She sets it on the table but doesn't apologize.

There's an age difference between us, and I'm really feeling it now.

"Have you been on a blind date before?" she asks.

"This is the first. You?"

"I've been on two. One ended with the guy ditching me at the restaurant, and the other one told me his last fling gave him genital warts." She studies me over the rim of her drink. "You're not going to do either one of those, are you?"

"No, ma'am." Jesus Christ.

She straightens in her chair. "I have something important to ask you."

"What's that?"

"It would make me really happy if you came to church with me on Sunday so you can meet my family."

I choke on my wine and end up in a coughing fit.

The server returns to take our orders, saving me from having to answer. I get a steak, and she orders the salmon.

"Thank you, sir. Ma'am." Gary takes our menus and retreats.

Zora immediately leans forward. "You really shouldn't eat red meat. It's bad for you."

"Is it?" I ask, not that I care for or want her opinion. Judging by the way her chin lifts and her eyes narrow, I think she gets the message. "So, tell me about yourself." Even as I ask, I know I don't have any genuine interest in her answer. I'm already done with this girl, but I'm stuck for the next hour.

"I'm an influencer. West Coast Style with Zora. Ever heard of it?"

"Can't say I'm on social media much."

"Oh." She looks at me like I'm a freak. "Well, I just passed a million followers."

"Impressive," I say. "I own a food truck. It's called Kyle's."

"A food truck?" Her lip curls. "Like one of those gross taco trucks?"

"Well, I sell other food. Maybe you could give it a try—tell your followers if you like the food."

"Yeah, that's not really the kind of thing my followers care about. They're much more upscale." She tilts her head. "You are cute, though. I'm sure I could use you in some of my posts. You'd be a big hit."

"Doing what?"

She shrugs. "Whatever I decide we're going to do for the day. Whatever's trending."

"I see." I take a sip of wine and glance around the room.

"I guess we should get this out of the way. If we're going to date, there are a few things you need to do," she says.

She's lost her mind. I can't wait to hear what she has to say. "Is that so?"

"Yes." Then she ticks them off on her fingers. "One. From now on, you'll need to dress in the clothing I pick out for you. But don't worry. I have excellent taste."

I'm speechless. Never in my life has a woman been so upfront and demanding. Is this really how dating is done these days? You show up with a plan and negotiate a list of demands and must-haves?

"Two. Remove any piercings if you have any I can't see." She gives a shudder. "They gross me out."

"What else, *darlin'*?" I play along.

"Three. I realize you have some tattoos. But I'm going to insist you don't get any more."

I nod. "No more tattoos. Check."

"Four. I'll need you to do several daily media posts with me for my business. You're really cute, and my followers will love you."

"Gee, that's one point for me, I suppose."

She finally picks up on my sarcasm. "If you can't do that, I'm afraid it's a deal-breaker."

"Anything else?"

"Yes. You're going to have to sell your food truck. They're tacky, and I can't be associated with someone who slings burgers and sells tacos out of a truck. Yuck."

"Tacky. Right." This is a joke—an elaborate joke the club set up. A tv host will jump out any minute and tell me I'm on a prank show. That doesn't seem to happen, though. People near us overhear our conversation and crane their necks, trying to get a look at me and see what's so awful that my date has just given me a list of things about myself I need to fix.

Once she completes her list, she sits back, sips her drink, and asks when I'll be able to get started. The server returns with our meals, and I have a lovely steak in front of me. So, now I'm contemplating dumping it on her and walking out.

"Would you like some more wine, sir?" the server asks.

"Definitely. Leave the bottle." I'll need enough to float a boat in order to get through this evening.

I struggle through the meal as she snaps photos of her plate and of herself moaning around each bite.

The food is fantastic, and I'm sitting at a table with a beautiful woman. From the outside, I suppose I must look like the luckiest man in the room.

And all I can think about is how much fun this would be if Sutton was here instead.

Finally, it comes time to pay the bill, I go to leave the tip, and Zora swipes it off the table in front of the server.

"People who serve aren't supposed to be tipped," she says with an elitist attitude that makes me cringe.

I take the money from her, hand it to the server, and stalk out of the restaurant without a goodbye, not even caring if she follows. Once outside, I get in my truck to leave.

Zora marches up to the window and taps on it. I power it down.

"Are we going to see each other again?"

"It amazes me you have the audacity to ask me that."

"Is that a yes?"

"Nope." I back out, leaving her with her mouth open.

As I drive home, I text Sutton.

ME: YOU WERE RIGHT.
SUTTON: ABOUT THE DATE? OH, NO.
ME: IT WAS A TRIP ON THE CRAZY TRAIN.

SUTTON: WHAT HAPPENED?

ME: SHE HAD A LIST FOR ME. THINGS SHE WANTED ME TO DO.

SUTTON: LIKE WHAT?

ME: GO TO CHURCH WITH HER, MEET HER FAMILY, LET HER DRESS ME FROM NOW ON. OH, AND GET THIS. SELL MY FOOD TRUCK BECAUSE THEY'RE—AND I QUOTE—"TACKY".

SUTTON: I TAKE IT YOU'RE NOT SEEING HER AGAIN.

ME: NOT A CHANCE

SUTTON: I SHOULDN'T ADMIT IT, BUT I'M GLAD.

I stare at her last text for a long time. I want to reply. I want to tell her how I wished it was her sitting across from me, but I don't feel safe putting it in writing where my brother might see.

ME: I'VE GOT THINGS TO DO WITH THE CLUB TOMORROW. I WON'T BE ABLE TO OPEN FOR BUSINESS

I wait for her reply, but it takes her a minute.

SUTTON: RAFE SAID THE SAME THING. SAID HE'LL BE OUT OF TOWN FOR MOST OF THE DAY.

I wonder if my brother has told her anything about where we're going or what we're doing. She never says more, and I don't reply. I drag a hand down my face, wishing I could call her, and we could talk. I even consider it for a moment, but instead, I drive home.

CHAPTER TWELVE

Kyle—

Last time the guys followed a truck, it took this route, so we're staked out behind the gas station where the truck and chase car fueled last time.

Cole thinks they've been doing this all this time, and no one's caught on, so probably they'll use the same route.

We stand around smoking, waiting for the tip off from Billy, who's lying up in the hills above the landing strip, positioned to give us the signal they're on the move.

Twenty minutes ago, the plane landed, and they unloaded.

"Should be anytime now," Cole says. A moment later, his phone goes off. He glances at the text. "They're on the move. Billy's gonna follow us when he's sure everyone has left the site."

Everyone is on this one tonight, except the prospects. Cole, Crash, Wolf, Red Dog, Green, Shane, Jake, TJ, Billy, Reckless, Marcus, Rafe, and me.

We lie in wait, our bikes hidden, and watch the truck and chase car arrive. While they're gassing up, Wolf slips off his cut and ruffles his hair up, then approaches the truck driver with a stooped gait.

He puts his hand out. "You got any change for an out of work veteran, man?"

"Get lost," the driver snaps.

Wolf shuffles away and I watch him dig the tracker from his pocket and stumble against the truck, attaching the magnet beneath it.

The driver comes around the back. "Get the hell out of here."

"I'm goin'. I'm goin'," Wolf mutters, his head down.

The two vehicles finish refueling, and pull out.

While we wait for Billy to catch up to us, Cole calls Daytona.

"Hey, brother. How are you?" Cole looks at the horizon. "Doin' well. Thanks. Hey, we've got a problem." He puts the call on speaker as Wolf comes around the corner and joins us.

"What's that?" Daytona replies.

Cole tells him about the connection to our attorney, and how we got on the trail that led us to these flights bringing in product that's being hauled to Vegas.

"No shit."

"They're transporting in a dump truck full of gravel. One's headed your way now. We managed to attach a tracker. We're gonna follow at a distance—keep about five miles back. We need to find out where it ends up and what happens. I don't want to lose it in Vegas traffic."

"Give me details. I'll try to pick it up and tail it."

"It's a green dump truck. Says *Smith Brothers Hauling* on the side. I can't find anything on the company."

"Probably bogus."

"That's my guess. I'll send you a link to our tracking app."

"That'd be great. I'll get on it now."

"One other thing, Daytona."

"What's that?"

"The name Warren Drake mean anything to you?"

"Can't say it does, but my VP has a lot of connections on the strip. I'll check into it, Cole."

"Thanks. See you soon."

Cole checks the app. "Looks like the truck is moving at about sixty miles an hour. They're eight miles ahead of us now. Let's maintain the interval. Mount up, boys."

We roar out of the gas station and haul ass down the interstate, then settle in at the same sixty mile per hour speed.

Every so often, we pull off on an exit ramp, and Cole checks to make sure the truck hasn't made a pit stop.

They stop in Bakersfield and again in Barstow. When they do, we exit before we get close and grab food and gas.

It's a long haul on our bikes, but eventually, we make it to Vegas. With all the stops, it's almost two in the afternoon when we hit town.

We pull over at a big gas station, and Cole calls Daytona and finds out he's on their tail in an unmarked van. We stay put until he finds out where the truck goes.

Thirty minutes later, Daytona calls back.

Cole picks up. "Yeah?"

They speak for about three minutes, Cole pacing away as he talks. When he finishes, he whistles and motions us over.

"They tracked them to a construction site north of town. Sign on the fence said Piedmont Developers."

"And?" Crash snaps.

"Piedmont Developers is a subsidiary of Sunrise Ltd. And that's owned by Barlow, Perkins, and Drake."

"Warren Drake?" Wolf mutters.

"Exactly. Come on. Daytona has some further information. We're meeting at their clubhouse."

We head north, far out of town until we're rolling down dirt roads in the desert. We finally reach the place, out in the middle of nowhere. It's elevated on a bit of a hill, and we climb the steps to the big, wide covered porch. We're led to the left and into a huge office that must take up half the building. Big windows overlook the view.

A couple of prospects carry in enough folding chairs for all of us, and then the door is closed, and we're left with Daytona, and his VP,

Trick.

Daytona sits behind his desk, his hands folded, looking troubled.

Cole and Crash are in the comfortable leather chairs in front of his desk, the rest of us positioned around in a half circle.

"This is a complicated story, boys. Warren Drake is really Carlo Bianchi, Jr," Daytona begins. "He's got a connection to the Santorini crime family. Took over when they got rid of their last guy. Trick had a run in with them a few years back. They are no one to mess with. They are the real deal."

"What kind of a run in?" Cole asks.

"Trick's ol' lady was a witness to one of their hits. They went after her. Trick had to go to New York to make a deal with them to spare her life. If your attorney stumbled upon their operation, they'd have gotten rid of him without thinking twice."

"Santorini?" Crash asks.

Daytona's eyes shift to him. "They're out of Jersey and New York. Franco is the head of the family. Guy named Fat Tony used to run the show here in Vegas."

"Used to?" Crash asks.

"The FBI used their leverage, and he was flipping on the family. Mob found out, and he turned up floating face down in the Las Vegas Wash."

"I thought the mob was finished in Vegas?" Green asks.

"They'd like us to believe that, but no. They are alive and well. They leave us alone, and we leave them alone."

"Until now," Cole says.

Daytona drags a hand down his face. "I can see where you think they're running up against us, moving in on our turf, but I'd let this go."

"They killed our attorney," Crash states.

"Get another one," Daytona replies, then looks at Trick. "Tell 'em, VP."

Trick leans against the edge of the desk. "No one gets to Franco Santorini. Everything goes through his man, Vito. I had the pleasure of dealing with them, like our prez told you. In my life, I've dealt with a lot of bad dudes, but these guys are a whole other level. We've got a tense truce between us, and it didn't come easy. They let us alone and we let them alone. Prez is right. You do not want to mess with these guys."

"They're running heroin through both our states," Cole snaps. "How is that staying out of our business?"

Daytona rubs his palms together and drops his head, then he leans back in his chair. "We haven't been in the heroin business since Taz went on a killing spree down in Temecula years ago, and you know it." He meets Cole's eyes. "Let this one go, brother. Or we'll all live to regret it."

Cole sucks in a long breath, his jaw clamping.

Every man in the room can tell how much this is costing him to let slide.

"Somebody's got to pay for Silver's death," he murmurs.

Daytona shakes his head. "I disagree. He was working a case that had nothing to do with club business. He fucked with the wrong people. That's on him. Let it go."

Crash looks at Cole. "Maybe he's right, brother. Two hundred grand is a lot of money, but it's not worth this kind of trouble."

"Two hundred grand?" Daytona frowns.

"His widow paid us to take out whoever killed her husband," Crash fills in.

"Jesus." Daytona shifts his eyes to Cole. "You in the murder-for-hire business all of a sudden?"

"It's more of a favor for a friend of the club." Cole stares off, his knee bouncing a mile a minute.

"Ain't no favor worth dying for, brother," Daytona advises.

Cole gets to his feet. "Let me think about it."

Daytona nods, not pressing for more.

And just like that, we all file out to the bar, still not sure where it stands.

Our chapter sidles up to the bar, grouped together and murmuring low.

"So, this goes right up the food chain to the mob," Crash hisses.

Cole nods. "And they're moving drugs right through our territory."

"We're fucked," Red Dog whispers.

"We've gone up against a lot of badasses, Cole. But the fucking mafia?" Green asks.

"I think the only way we do this is if we can make a statement under the radar, without them knowing it's us," Cole muses.

"This is the mafia, Prez. *The mafia*," Green reiterates. "Cement shoes, floating with the fishes, the Godfather."

"I know who the mafia is, Green," Cole snaps.

Red Dog points a finger at our prez. "You are out of your mind, brother."

"I can't let this lie, Dog."

"For what? For Harry Silver's widow? For two hundred grand? It's not worth it. You'll put a death warrant on every single one of our backs. Daytona's crew, too." Red Dog drags a hand down his jaw.

Cole drains his whiskey glass. "We'll head home in the morning. I'm calling Church the minute we get back. We'll talk about it there."

The older members are pissed. It's clear on their faces they think retaliation is insane. I exchange a glance with the rest of us younger guys. They look shell-shocked and apprehensive, but if Cole gives the order, every one of us will head to our bikes and climb on like obedient soldiers.

"Let's play a game of pool," TJ suggests.

I follow, dreading what's coming and ruing the day Harry Silver's widow pulled onto our clubhouse ground.

CHAPTER THIRTEEN

Kyle—

When we return to our clubhouse, the ol' ladies are waiting.

I climb from my bike slowly, stretching my aching muscles. The tiredness goes to my bones, but a little shot of adrenaline hits my veins when I spot Sutton in the crowd.

Our eyes lock, and she gives me a little wave.

God, I want to run to her and sweep her in my arms, but she's not my girl.

My brother reiterates that thought by doing what I long to do. He twirls her around, then sets her down and gives her ass a swat. His arm hooks around her shoulders, and he steers her inside.

I hang back and light a smoke, in no rush.

My father stops beside me as the crowd thins, everyone else heading through the door.

"How are you doing, son?"

"Tired."

He grins. "Can I bum a smoke?"

I shake one out for him, then flick my lighter, and he dips his head. Once it's lit, he blows smoke toward the sky.

"We having Church now?" I ask.

"God, I hope not. I want to get home. I'm exhausted."

"What do you think Prez is going to do about this whole Santorini situation?"

"I don't know. I hope he comes to his senses. I sure don't want a war with the mob."

Just the thought that one wrong move and that's where this thing could go is chilling. "Something like that starts, I don't think there'll be any way to stop it."

Wolf stares at the horizon. "It'd be like a runaway freight train, barreling toward the station."

"Dad?" I meet my father's eyes. "You've got to talk him out of this."

"I know. Crash and Red Dog are in there right now, trying to make him see it would be insane to go down this road."

"You think they can do it?"

"I don't know. I've never seen Cole back down when it comes to someone fucking with the club."

"It's not just us, Dad. This would drag every chapter in the country into this war. Over what? A two-bit lawyer we didn't even like much?"

"It's more than that. It's disrespecting the MC. Our territory."

"I think the mob thinks Vegas is *their* territory. I think they think it's been theirs since the forties."

Car tires on gravel draw my attention, and I tap my father's arm and lift my chin to the Mercedes pulling in.

"Silver's widow. Goddamn it," my father hisses and flings his cigarette. "Go deal with her."

I grind my butt under my boot and stroll over to the car, shoving my hands in my pockets. Before I reach the driver door, she's throwing the car in park and climbing out. Then she's stalking toward me, and I'm walking backward in front of her, my hands out.

"Can I help you, Mrs. Silver?"

"Yes, get out of my way," she snaps, trying to side-step around me, but I dart to the side, blocking her.

"What do you need?" I stall, hoping my father will come to my aid.

"I want to talk to Cole. Now."

I glance at Pops, and he nods.

"Okay, let me take you to him. Follow me." I hold the door for her, and she sails past me, her expensive perfume billowing in her wake. She's got on a caramel-colored coat with a matching fur color, a tight black skirt, tall boots, and enough gold jewelry to fill a bucket.

I lead her across the clubhouse toward the hall, aware of the eyes of every brother in the club, all twisted on their bar stools. Even the pool players pause the game to watch.

We go down the hall to his office, and I tap on the door.

"Yeah?" Cole's voice calls.

I open the door. "You got a visitor, Prez."

Before I can say more, she pushes past me, and Cole springs to his feet.

"Joselyn."

"Have you found anything?" she asks, her voice all soft and sweet for our prez.

Crash and Red Dog sit in the two chairs in front of the desk. Crash offers her his seat.

"Sit down, sweetheart."

"I'm not your sweetheart," she snaps, then calms her tone. "I'm sorry. Thank you. That was kind. I'm just an emotional wreck." Her eyes return to Cole. "Did you catch them?"

"Not exactly."

No one tells me to get out, so I stick around.

"What does that mean?" she asks.

"We think Harry found out something that got him killed," Crash says.

Her gaze moves to him and back to our prez. "What kind of thing?"

Cole looks to Crash, and his expression reads, *how much do we tell her?*

Crash shifts. "He, ah, may have stuck his nose into some shit, sorry, stuff he should have left alone."

"What kind of thing?" she repeats.

Cole strokes his chin with the back of his hand and finally exhales. "The mob, Joselyn. He found out some things they were doing—illegal things—and we think that's what the trip to Vegas was about. We think he confronted the wrong people, and it got him killed."

"Who? I want a name," she says.

"The Santorini Crime Family," I say.

"Kyle," Cole snaps, shutting me up.

Her head swivels to me and then back to Cole. "You're serious, aren't you? The actual mafia?"

"Serious as a heart attack," Cole replies.

She lowers into the chair Crash vacated. "I can't believe this. Why would he get involved with anything to do with them?"

"We think it was an accident. He stumbled upon a drop-off site— a place they were using to move drugs into the country."

"But why would he go to Vegas?"

Cole shrugs. "We're not sure. We may never know what went down."

"Who's the head guy?" she asks.

"In Jersey?" Crash asks.

"No. In Vegas. Is it that Warren Drake man? He put the hit on my baby?"

"We've been told Warren Drake is actually Carlo Bianchi, Jr. According to our sources, the Santorinis installed him in Vegas when the last guy, Fat Tony, ended up floating face down." Cole tilts his head, and his eyes narrow on Joselyn. "Don't get any crazy ideas, Joselyn. These are not the kind of people you mess with."

"Are you going to take care of it?"

"We're not going up against the mob for you," Crash snaps, pissed off.

"VP," Cole barks.

But Crash doesn't stop. "Harry is dead and gone, Mrs. Silver. None of this will bring him back. The only thing it will do is get someone else killed. Is that what you want?"

Cole pinches the bridge of his nose, his eyes closing, looking tired and frustrated. "We've been trying to come up with a way to get a little payback that doesn't end up with anyone else getting whacked by the mob."

"Have you come up with anything?" she asks.

"Not yet."

She stares at the floor, and we can all see the wheels turning.

Cole leans his elbows on the desk. "Don't even think about it, Joselyn."

Her eyes shift to him.

"I'm serious, woman. This is not Ocean's Eleven. You are no match against these guys."

"Maybe you don't know me very well. Maybe I'm the perfect person to go up against them. Maybe they'll never suspect me."

"Jesus Christ." Crash flings a hand out. "Are you hearing this, Prez?"

"Honey," Red Dog starts, taking her hand. "It's too dangerous. It's a nice thought that you want to avenge your husband like this. I mean that. It's real admirable, but we can't allow it."

Her brows lift. "Can't allow it?"

Cole's head drops. "Shit, Dog. Those are fighting words. You're married. You should know that."

"Okay, sorry. Poor choice of words. But don't be insane."

Cole slumps back and stares at the ceiling. "Now you're calling her insane, Dog."

"I didn't mean that. We don't want your blood on our hands."

"My blood wouldn't be on your hands," she replies.

"If we don't stop you, it sure will feel like it," Cole agrees. Then he pulls open a drawer and brings out a bottle and a handful of shot glasses. "Here. Let's drink to Harry. You know he wouldn't want you putting yourself in danger."

Cole fills them and passes them out. Then lifts his in the air. "To Harry. Best attorney we ever had, and a good husband."

She looks torn, but she drinks and sets her shot glass on the desk. "I want my money back."

Cole nods, reaches into a drawer, and drops the fat envelope on the desk.

She swipes it and stands, shoving it in her purse.

Cole rises to his feet. "You're not going to do anything, are you?"

She doesn't reply, then turns. I step out of her way, opening the door for her. Once her heels are clicking down the hall, I look back at Prez.

"She's gonna be trouble," he mutters.

"But not our trouble," Red Dog says.

"Depends if the mob found out we've been sniffing around. She could make it look like we're to blame for whatever she's concocting in that pretty blonde head." Cole lifts his chin at Crash. "We're gonna need to keep tabs on her movements. Set up a schedule. Rotate the prospects and some of the other guys. I want to know where she goes."

"On it. You got another one of them trackers?" Crash asks him.

Cole digs in his top drawer and tosses one on the desk.

Crash snags it and turns to me. "Come on, kid."

I follow him out the door, thankful, at least, the club isn't putting a hit on Carlo Bianchi.

"That was close," I whisper.

Crash frowns. "It ain't over yet. I need you to stall her long enough for me to put this on her car. Think you can handle that?"

"Sure." I trot ahead, catching up to her just as she's opening her car door. "Hey, darlin'."

She turns her blue eyes on me, giving me a quizzical look, her gaze traveling over me. "Yes? What is it?"

I give her a dazzling smile. "I'm sorry about how Prez treated you. I think it's real sweet how you want to take out these guys. I wish I had an ol' lady who wouldn't hesitate to kill a man for me." Out of my peripheral vision, I see Crash come out the door and head to his bike. I sidle closer to her and make sure she's turned away from the rear of her car.

He doubles back and moves slowly toward her bumper.

The gravel under his boots crunch, and Joselyn starts to turn.

Thinking quickly, I lift a hand to cup her cheek, keeping her eyes on me. "Harry was a lucky man to have such a beautiful, devoted woman like you." I'm pouring it on thick because Crash is taking his sweet time.

Joselyn shoves my hand away. "Are you hitting on me?"

Finally, he heads back to his bike, and I straighten, shoving my hands in my pockets. "No, ma'am."

She shakes her head and climbs in her car. "Good grief."

I stand there and watch her peel out, gravel flying.

Crash approaches me with a big grin on his face. "You dog. Hitting on the widow."

"It was all I could think to do. You took your sweet time, by the way."

"Well, when I heard you pouring it on so thick, I had to smoother my laughter. You into cougars, Kyle?"

"Bite me," I snap and head to the door, my VP's laughter following me inside.

CHAPTER FOURTEEN

Kyle—

The following day, Sutton and I work the lunch and dinner rush at the Farmer's Market. When we finish and close up, my phone goes off.

RAFE: CAN YOU BRING SUTTON TO THE CLUBHOUSE AND I'LL PICK HER UP THERE?
ME: I CAN, BUT IT'LL HAVE TO BE ON MY BIKE. I'M NOT HAULING THE TRAILER ALL THE WAY TO THE CLUBHOUSE AND I'M NOT UNHITCHING IT TONIGHT.
RAFE: FINE. JUST MEET ME AT THE CLUBHOUSE

"What is it?" Sutton asks, glancing at my phone.

"Rafe wants me to give you a ride to the clubhouse. Said he'll pick you up there after I drop the trailer off at my place."

"Okay."

I'm not sure she even knows the significance of this, but if Rafe is good with it, I'll take any chance I can to spend more time with her.

I lock up the food truck, and we climb into my pickup and haul it to my house, where I plan to leave it parked for the night.

"That was her. I'm sure of it." Sutton picks up the conversation we'd been having earlier.

"The lady in the baseball cap and sunglasses?" I ask, glancing over. "I doubt it."

"It was her. I've heard she wears disguises sometimes, so she gets to give an honest opinion."

"Well, she did order three different items." I hang my wrist over the steering wheel and watch the reflection of the streetlights flash across the windshield.

"Exactly. She got the chicken chili, cornbread, the onion rings, and a cheeseburger. I watched her sit at one of the picnic tables. She tasted everything, then made notes on her phone after each bite. Then she dumped the rest in the trash and left."

I lift a brow. "She threw my food away. That can't be good."

"Food critics do that. They can't possibly eat everything they review."

"If you say so."

In a few minutes, I pull into my driveway and park. We climb out and head to my bike. The neighborhood is quiet, crickets chirping in the night air.

I dig my spare helmet out of my saddlebag and hand it over.

Putting Sutton on the back of my bike is a dream come true. It's not something I would ever normally do, because brothers don't haul around another member's girl on the back of their bike. That's sacred. But I can only assume Rafe knew just what he was asking when he said it.

She climbs on the back and wraps her arms around me, holding on tight. It feels good. It feels right.

As we drive across town, I don't want it to end, so I take the long way.

Finally, I pull into the clubhouse lot, and we climb off. I lead her to the bar, and we take two stools. "You think she liked the food? The Five Forks lady," I clarify.

Sutton grins. "How could she not? She'll give your food Five Forks for sure."

Green turns from his stool. "Some chick giving you forks? Is that like one of them dating app winks?"

I chuckle, and Sutton explains. "It's like getting five stars. It's a way of reviewing his food."

"Huh. How 'bout that?" Green stands, reaches over the bar top, and grabs a handful of forks. "Here. I'll give you five forks."

Sutton rolls her eyes. "That's not how it works."

"Don't bother trying to explain it to him, Sutton. He's yankin' my chain."

"Oh." She turns to Green. "His food is very good, you know."

"I do know. I ate a bunch at the picnic." He looks at me. "I told ya I liked it, didn't I?"

"Yeah, Green. You did."

"What's goin' on?" TJ asks, walking up.

"Kyle's collecting forks," Green replies.

TJ glances over at me. "The fork lady come try your food?"

"Sutton thinks she saw her today. I'm not so sure it was her," I say.

"It was her," she insists.

I order us a couple of beers, and Sutton checks her phone.

"Nothing yet. She usually posts her daily reviews by nine."

Cole, Crash, and TJ walk over and take a stool at the bar.

"What are you boys up to?" Crash asks.

Green lifts his chin to me. "Kyle and Sutton just got here." He slides a fork across the bar to Crash. "Here. Give him a fork."

Crash frowns at me. "Is he high?"

I shrug. "He's just being Green."

"What the fuck's he talking about?" Cole asks.

"Never mind. It's a stupid joke," TJ tells his ol' man.

Green points a fork at me. "Hey. My jokes are never stupid."

The prospect behind the bar carries over two long necks, and I tilt mine up. Sutton continues to check her phone.

I shake my head. "Don't waste all night on that."

"I can't help it. I have to know."

I lock eyes with TJ. "Heard from Brayden lately?"

"He talked to Ma a couple of days ago. She said he sounded happy." TJ gets a beer. "He texted me last week. I think he misses Cali, but he loves that girl too much to drag her from her home and family. He'll stick it out."

"Any plans to come home for a visit?" I rest a hand on the bar top and turn to talk to him.

TJ shrugs. "Maybe over the summer."

Marcus and Brandy, and Billy and Melissa walk in, followed by my brother.

The girls hug Sutton.

"Hey, girl," Melissa says, then looks at me. "Did you guys work today?"

"We did. Just finished the dinner rush."

Sutton checks her phone again. "It's up!" She quickly scans through it. "It's about us!"

I lean over her shoulder. "What does it say?"

She reads it aloud.

I'd heard about Kyle's *as many of you have tagged me in your own reviews of the new food truck making waves in San Jose. Plus, the videos of customers raving about them have gone viral. So, with high expectations, I headed across the Bay Bridge to check them out for myself.*

I have to say that Kyle's *serves up what is by far the best chicken chili I've ever had, and the onion rings are to die for. As a bonus, they come with an amazing secret sauce that was a gift to my pallet. Their cheeseburgers are cooked to perfection with a fantastic bakery bun, elevating it beyond the usual fare served around town.*

You can try them for yourself outside the Farmer's Market at San Pedro Square every Tuesday and Thursday, plus varying spots around the city. Their daily locations can be found on their website, which I've listed below.

In my humble opinion, Kyle's *is definitely worth the trip across the Bay Bridge.*

Five Fantastic Forks!

Sutton throws her fists in the air and bounces on her feet, then hugs me. I'm grinning from ear to ear, filled with stunned amazement and joy, but my eyes connect with Rafe, and I quickly disengage.

"Congrats, man," Marcus says, clasping my hand. "I take it this is a big deal?"

"*Huge.*" Sutton fills him in. "A good review from this lady is like magic fairy dust. She can make or break a career with one review."

"Well, that's a great review, Kyle," Melissa says, and hugs my neck. When she pulls back, she pats my arm. "Well deserved, too." She turns to her father. "We should celebrate."

Cole raises his glass of whiskey. "Cheers to ya, Kyle. I'm happy for you."

"I know," Brandy says, snapping her fingers and looking at Melissa and Sutton. "We should go up to the marina, where my father has his boat. I'm sure he'll let us use it."

"Or we could ride the bikes down to the beach," Billy suggests. "I've been wanting to check out Pacifica."

"Either way, I see bikinis in our future," Marcus replies with a grin.

"Oh, let's go to the beach. They've got that pier, and I've always wanted to check out that taco place on the beach. I've heard they've got awesome frozen margaritas," Sutton says.

"I'm sold," Green chimes in.

TJ tilts his head. "What do you think, Dad? You want to make it a club ride?"

Cole turns to Crash. "You up for it, VP?"

Crash shrugs. "Sure."

Cole downs his beer and stands. "Okay. Sunday good for you?"

Seeing Sutton's happiness, I can't help but agree. "Sure."

"We'll head out at eleven on Sunday." He lifts a chin to Crash. "Come back to the office with me."

I watch them walk out and catch Green's eyes. "I'm surprised he agreed to that."

"Anything that takes his mind off starting a war with the mob, I'm all for," he replies, tilting his beer up.

"Amen," I murmur.

Sunday morning, I roll into the clubhouse lot at eleven am on the dot. Most of the club is already here. Shane and Briana, Jake and Layla, Crash and Shannon, Cole and Angel. I park next to Rafe and Sutton and climb from my bike.

Rafe sits sideways on his seat, yawns, and then sips from his coffee. "Who's idea was this?"

"Your girl's, dumbass," I rib him.

"Oh." He holds his cup up. "Great idea, babe. Yay."

Sutton rolls her eyes and turns her attention to me. "How long do you think it'll take us?"

"It's just under an hour ride to get up there."

"Where's TJ and Gigi?" Billy asks, walking over with Melissa, holding hands like they're high-school sweethearts.

I slip my phone from my pocket. "I don't know. Let me call him." A moment later, I've got him on speaker. "Where are you, brother?"

"In bed. Gettin' my dick sucked. Why?"

I laugh, my eyes on the horizon. "We're all assembled in the clubhouse parking lot, ready to head out."

"Shit. I forgot." Then a muffled, "Babe, hurry up."

Cole walks up, his arm around Angel. "Where's TJ?"

"You better haul ass down here, TJ. Prez wants to know where you are," I add.

He hangs up, and I grin at Cole. "He's comin'."

"Literally." Billy smirks, and Melissa whacks his arm.

Cole's eyes shift between us. "He's got ten minutes, then we're leavin' without him."

"Aw, come on, Daddy," Melissa pleads. "You wouldn't leave your daughter-in-law behind, would you?"

He sighs. "Fine. But they better hurry." He and Angel head inside.

"He loves Gigi," Melissa says.

"There's Wolf and Crystal." Billy lifts his chin, and I turn toward my mother and father, pulling in, Green and Sara behind them.

"And there are your parents," I reply as Red Dog and Mary bring up the rear.

My eyes shift to Sutton, and she smiles at me. I have to settle for that. I'm learning to live off whatever time I can spend near her, knowing it's all I'll ever have from this girl. Just a meeting of the eyes and a smile. It has to be enough.

I'm the odd man out today—the only one without a woman riding bitch. It's never bothered me before, but today it does. I know it's going to be hard to keep my eyes off Sutton.

Soon TJ and Gigi arrive, and we pull out in formation. Since I'm solo, I take the rear. I find Rafe and Sutton two rows ahead, her chin resting on his shoulder. He reaches back and strokes her thigh. Looking away, my jaw tightens.

An hour later, we park our bikes in a lot near the beach and walk over. Several of the girls have brought blankets to spread out in the sand, and they shimmy out of their jeans and shirts until they're down to their bikinis. Someone brought a frisbee, and soon they've got a game going.

I strip my boots and shirt and join in. I prefer that to watching Rafe rub sunscreen on Sutton's smooth skin.

When the sun gets too hot, we wade into the waves.

An hour later, Green emits a sharp whistle and motions with his arm, then cups his hands around his mouth. "Margarita time. Let's go."

We make our way to the taco place on the beach and sit out on the deck overlooking the ocean.

Rafe is slow in coming out with his and Sutton's drinks, and she sits next to me, saving the chair on her other side for my brother.

Green sips on a frozen mango margarita, then looks over at Cole. "Why don't we have one of these machines at the clubhouse? We could have frozen margaritas whenever we want."

"You feel free to buy us one, Green."

He scans his phone. "A thousand bucks? Jesus."

"That's why we don't have one," Cole says, sipping on his own.

Angel leans against his side. "We should come up here sometime and visit that place we once stayed at, remember?"

Cole dips his head, rubbing his jaw against her forehead. "You mean that place in Rockaway, overlooking the water?"

She nods. "That's the one. And we could eat at Nick's. I loved that place."

"Sure, baby doll. You figure out a weekend, and we'll do it." He kisses her forehead and squeezes her thigh.

"I want a love like they have," Sutton whispers, and I turn toward her.

"It's lasted decades, and there's nothing gonna pull those two apart," I reply.

Rafe walks up and passes her a frozen strawberry margarita, then takes his seat and looks at the view, kicking his legs out. "This is the life, huh?"

"Yep, this is the life," I reply, glancing at Sutton, and she smiles. I turn my attention to the ocean and listen to the waves rolling on the beach's edge. Seagulls float in the wind and play amid the glittering white waves. I feel myself unwind in the warmth of the sun.

A moment later, my phone goes off. I don't recognize the number, and let it go, setting it on the table. A minute later, it dings, notifying me I have a voicemail. I frown and put it to my ear.

Then I set the phone down and stare at Sutton.

Seeing my expression, she frowns. "What is it?"

My mouth drops open. "They just offered me a spot at Tribe."

"What's Tribe?" she asks.

Green answers for me. "Tribe is awesome. It's that music festival out in the Mohave desert. I went there when I was a youngster like you. I don't know if it still does, but back then, that thing lasted a week."

"Now it's three days."

Sutton turns to me. "They offered you a spot for the food truck?"

"That was one of the festival organizers. He saw the review." I meet her eyes. "Do you know how hard it is to get a spot at Tribe?"

"That's awesome, bro. Congratulations," Rafe says.

I toss my phone on the table. "I can't go."

"Why not?" Green asks.

"I'd never be able to run the truck by myself. The crowds are epic there."

Green lifts his chin to Sutton. "So, take her. She works for ya, don't she?"

I meet Rafe's eyes.

He appears caught off guard.

Green notices the vibe that passes between us. "Aw, come on, man. This is his dream. You gonna stand in his way?"

"I guess not," Rafe replies. "If she wants to go, that's up to her."

Sutton's jaw works, and I'm not sure she likes his answer.

I shake the remnants of the frozen drink in the bottom of my plastic cup and toss it back, then stand. "I'm gonna get another one." I head inside. Green tears into Rafe as I go.

"Don't be a dick, Rafe. You know how hard he's worked. This is his shot."

"I said she could go, didn't I?"

I walk into the building and stand in line. A moment later, I feel a presence at my side. It's Sutton.

"I'll come with you," she offers.

"You sure?" I ask, wondering if I should even consider taking her up on her offer. Traveling alone with her—it's insane to think about. Yet I find the words tumbling out of my mouth. "It's a three-day festival."

She bites her lip. "This is your big shot. We have to do it. So, do we camp?"

Green comes in from the deck and walks over to us, his eyes hitting Sutton. "You goin' with him?"

"Yes."

"She's concerned about sleeping in a tent," I tell him.

"I didn't say that exactly."

"Sara and I have a camper. We bought it two years ago so we could go to the Grand Canyon. You can take that."

"A camper?" I ask. "What kind?"

He pulls out his phone and shows me a picture. "It's built on the chassis of a Ford 350. It's 22ft long, and there's a trailer hitch so you can pull your food trailer. There are two couches on either side that fold down to beds."

"Is there a bathroom?" Sutton asks.

"Yep, even a small shower and kitchenette. AC, heat… everything you need."

"You sure you want me to take that? It looks expensive as hell," I say.

"It was. Sara's father chipped in. He's big into RVing and wanted us to get into it, too."

"How'd that work out?" I ask with a grin.

"Hey, I dig it. Just don't have a lot of time for it lately."

"Are you seriously offering this thing, Green? That's a big deal."

"Absolutely. It'll be perfect for what you need, and I'm happy it'll get some use."

I look at Sutton. "What do you think?"

"Let's do it."

Green grins and taps her chin with a wink. "Thatta girl." His attention shifts to me. "You got a chance to make some good money at this thing. Maybe even enough to start up a real brick and mortar restaurant."

Sutton frowns and searches my eyes. "Is that your dream? A real restaurant?"

I shrug. "I mean, if this thing takes off, it'd be nice to get out of that trailer."

Green clamps a hand on my shoulder. "This is a great opportunity for you, Kyle. I hope everything works out." His eyes shift between Sutton and me, and I get the feeling he's talking about more than just the festival.

CHAPTER FIFTEEN

Kyle—

I open the door as boots stomp up my steps. Green stands there, twirling a set of keys on his finger.

"All right, here's the Love Machine." He tosses the keys to me.

"Love Machine?" I smirk. "Please tell me it's got clean sheets. Or do I need to buy a black light?"

"I would not recommend that." Green winks. "But yeah, it has clean sheets in the cabinet above one of the pullout couches."

"Got it. Anything else I need to know?"

"Follow me. I'll give you a quick tour."

I trail behind him as he climbs into the RV.

"These couches pull out. You lift these arm rests out and then pull it down."

I watch as he maneuvers one of the couches into a bed, leaving barely any room.

"You said it had two beds," I grumble, realizing these two practically form a king bed.

"There's an aisle."

"The size of my credit card?"

"Well, you're not planning to make a move on your brother's girl, are you?" Green snips.

"Hell no. But would you want me riding off with Sarah in this thing?"

"No, but I'm in a serious relationship with Sarah." He wiggles his ring finger at me.

"Rafe and Sutton aren't serious?"

"Would you have let your girl go off with your brother on a three-day trip where they share an RV?" He raises his brows.

"You're the one who was giving him shit about letting her come," I defend.

"Yeah, 'cause that's my job. Besides, none of you little shits listen to a word I say, anyway. If he was really into her, he'd have come himself."

That gives me pause. Green seems to know he made his point and moves on with the tour.

"Here's the bathroom."

I poke my head in, noting the sink, toilet, and enclosed shower.

"The generator runs off the gas tank. When it gets down to a fourth a tank of gas, it shuts off, so you don't get stuck somewhere. Speaking of not getting stuck anywhere… there's some wood in this cabinet." He moves to the couches, lifting one of the cabinet doors to reveal sheets of plywood. "Use these if it rains. I don't want my baby getting stuck in the mud."

"We're going to the desert. I don't think we'll be seeing any rain."

"You never know, kid. Well, I think that covers everything."

We move down the steps. Sarah waves at me through the windshield of the SUV she waits in.

"What's this ladder for?" I gesture to a ladder going up the back.

"Oh, the roof is walkable."

"Nice."

"Well, gotta go. Mia's got a soccer game today."

"Isn't she only like four?"

"Three. They kick the ball around with basically blowup bumpers around the field. It's really just watching a bunch of toddlers run back and forth. But my girl is going to kick ass."

"I wouldn't expect anything less from your little girl."

"Damn right. Good luck, kid. Make some money."

"Thanks, Green."

He climbs in the SUV

As he pulls away, I walk through the RV, taking in the two sofas. This is such a bad idea. We'll practically be sleeping in the same bed. I shake the thoughts from my head. Tribe is the opportunity of a lifetime. I need to stay focused on that. This could be my big break, and there's no room for me to fuck it all up by letting my thoughts of Sutton get in the way. I cannot let myself fall for this girl.

Rafe drops Sutton off about an hour later as I'm getting the food trailer hitched to the RV.

The breath whooshes out of me as I rise.

She's in a pair of cutoffs that show her slender, tanned legs that go on and on for miles. She has a loose-fitting white shirt with a generous plunging neckline and some kind of loose, pale green cover up.

I quickly avert my eyes when Rafe approaches, a duffel slung over his arm.

He carries her bag into the camper.

I tense, waiting for the hell-raising I'm sure will come if he notices the couch-bed layout. But when he steps out, he seems unfazed.

"Hey, man. Good luck." He pats my back, then turns to Sutton and pecks her on the cheek. "Have a fun time, but not too fun." Then gives a small wave to us both, climbs into his truck, and drives away.

I can't help but think if my girl was going off for several days, I'd have given her a hell of a lot more than a peck on the cheek. But then again, maybe they said their real goodbyes this morning. It's not my business, so I shake the image from my mind and push back the jealousy surging through me.

Clearing my throat, I glance over at Sutton. "Ready?"

"Yes, let's make you a famous chef." She gives me a brilliant smile and climbs into the passenger side.

I huff a laugh, realizing just how excited I am to spend time with her. "How about we just sell some food?"

"Sure thing. How long is this trip, anyway?"

"Including stops, it should take us about five hours to get to the Mojave Desert. Thankfully, Tribe is held on the California side." I drop the gearshift into drive and roll onto the street.

"Well, good thing I brought travel snacks." Sutton lifts a large purse onto her lap and begins taking out Cheez-its, M&Ms, little packages of donuts, a can of Pringles, and a bag of miniature cookies.

"Jesus, did you rob a junk food store?"

"Ha ha. Half the fun of traveling is eating all the cheat food. It's basic knowledge calories don't count on a road trip."

Now she has me belly-laughing. "Okay, pass me some Cheez-its, then."

She hands them over, and I tear into them.

"I pulled up a list of the lineup and made a playlist. That way, we can decide if we want to sneak off to watch anyone after we shut down each night. Oh, and one of my favorite bands is going to be there, so I'm kind of stoked."

I glance over, her excitement contagious. She really is a ray of sunshine. "Who's your favorite band?"

"Whiskey Mirage."

"No kidding? I love those guys."

"Awesome! We can go see them together." She crunches on a Pringle as she hooks her phone to the RV's Bluetooth.

Soon music blasts through the speakers.

She dances along, and warmth spreads through my chest. This girl is a perfect catch. I bite my cheek. *Focus.* I tamp down those feelings and tell myself for the thousandth time, *she's your brother's girlfriend.* She's off limits. But damn, does being with her feel right.

We roll into the festival grounds around four and observe a sea of tents and cars. I flash the permit they sent me in the mail and drive through, looking for my spot amongst the other venders.

"There's twenty-eight." Sutton points to an open area with a yard sign labeling it.

After parking, we climb from the vehicle.

"Hey, why don't you go check things out, and I'll get everything prepped for tonight?" I suggest.

"Are you sure?" she asks, already walking backward away from me.

I grin, because she's obviously taking me up on it. "I'm sure."

"Thanks, boss man," she calls over her shoulder and takes off for a booth selling jewelry nearby.

I could tell she wanted to check out the vendors, but that's not the real reason I told her to go. After being stuck in the same car for the last six hours, I need some time away from her. I need to distance myself so I can get my head screwed on straight. *She's taken, Kyle. She's your brother's girl.*

I repeat the mantra over and over in my head as I prep the ingredients I need for tonight's dinner rush.

I almost have myself convinced I have no feelings for her when she walks in, carrying a small bag.

"Already spending money?" I chide.

"Just a necklace I liked."

I nod and go back to chopping.

A few moments later, she slides next to me. "What's on the menu?"

My eyes are drawn to the necklace now dangling around her throat. It consists of two gold chains, one at a regular length and the other dipping low, right to the top of her cleavage, where a sage-colored desert glass pendant rests. Her breasts look full, and I ache to touch them. My heart beats a mile a minute as I try to think of the question she just asked.

"Ahem," I clear my throat. "Is that your new necklace?"

She looks down. "Yeah. Do you like it?"

"It's nice."

"So… is the menu a secret?"

"What? No." *That* was her question. "We're going to make all the hits—cheeseburgers, onion rings, chicken chili, and cornbread."

"Great, I'll go write it on the chalkboard."

The first night we have quite a crowd. I rack in as much money as I do in a week in San Jose. Sutton handles the customers like a pro, so I can focus on cranking out the food. We work together like a well-oiled machine. I can't help but wonder if we would work this well in other ways.

CHAPTER SIXTEEN

Sutton—

"Ready to head out?" Kyle asks as I apply some lip gloss.

"So ready. I can't wait to hear some music." I shimmy my hips and giggle.

Kyle extends his hand to help me from the RV. It feels good to be in the fresh air, away from the food truck.

We pass several other vendors, noting what the competition is selling and pointing at their menu items. We make our way to the closest of five stages.

Kyle grabs us a couple of beers, and we weave through the crowd until we're only a few rows of people back from the stage.

I dance to the music, feeling the beat run through me. I sashay my hips and roll my stomach to the rhythm, twirling my hands and beer over my head. Kyle bops his head to the beat, and I even catch a few toe taps.

He looks sexy as hell in the gray t-shirt stretched across his pecs. His muscular, tattooed arms are on full display.

I try not to look. I'm with Rafe, and Kyle has no interest in me. He made that clear from the first time we met. I gave him the opening, and he passed me along to his twin. Not that Rafe hasn't been a fun time, but the spark—the chemistry—it isn't what it should be.

We dance through the set, yelling over the music until our voices are hoarse.

After a couple of hours, Kyle shouts over the music. "Want to head back?"

"Sure."

"Should we grab a bite? I'm starving," he yells in my ear.

I nod, and we move through the crowd.

After stopping at another truck that stayed open late, we head to the camper.

"Want to sit on the roof?" he asks, gesturing to the ladder.

"We can sit on the roof?" My voice buzzes with excitement. "Sign me up."

He smiles. "All right, pass me the food. I don't want you falling because your hands are full."

As I climb up, Kyle disappears into the camper, only to emerge a few minutes later with a folded blanket.

"Now who has their hands full?" I tease from the roof.

"I'll manage," he calls up as he ascends the ladder.

After spreading the blanket, we take a seat and dive into our food.

"Goodness, check out all those stars. I've never seen so many." I gaze at the sky. "It's like someone spilled glitter across black velvet."

"Yeah, no light pollution to dim them."

When we finish eating, we lie back on the blanket and stare at the sky.

We gaze at the stars for a long time before either of us speaks again.

"You did amazing today. I think word will spread, and you'll do even better tomorrow." I turn my head to look over at him.

"I hope so."

"Kyle, a shooting star!" I point to the streak of light flashing across the sky. "We should make a wish."

I close my eyes and let my heart speak my wish to the heavens. Then I glance over at Kyle again. "What'd you wish for?"

"I can't tell you," he chastises. "It won't come true."

"Wow." I giggle. "I did *not* have you pegged for the superstitious type."

"I'm not, but I'm still not telling." His laughter rumbles, and warmth spreads through me at the sound.

"Well, tell me something else, then. Do you really want a restaurant? Like a building?"

"Yeah, I mean, that's the end goal. I'd love to have my own place. Hopefully a thriving one, where I could have multiple locations."

"That's a good dream. I think you'll get there."

"What about you?" He turns and pins me with those gorgeous, warm eyes. "What's your dream? What do you want to do?"

"Nope." I shake my head. "Not telling."

"Why not?"

"You'll think it's stupid." I suddenly feel vulnerable.

"I'd never think someone's dream was stupid." His eyes pierce into mine.

"Fine, but it's not big or typical."

"Stop downplaying your dream. If it's what you want, say it. Be proud of it. Then go after it."

"Okay, okay. I want to have a family business."

His brows furrow. "Do your parents own something?"

"No. I mean my own family—the one I want to start."

"Really?"

I nod. "I'm ready to settle down. And I want my family to do something where we work together. We set our own time. We build something together. I've always thought it would be fun to work with my spouse and have our kids running around, causing mischief."

"That's not a stupid dream. Though, I have to say most people don't want to work with their spouse."

"I want mine to be my best friend—the person I want to tell first when something great happens or something terrible. And I've always wanted to work with my best friend."

He clears his throat like he's nervous. "Good thing you've got Rafe. Maybe you should work with him instead of me."

When I think of my dream, Rafe is not who I imagine beside me. He's not my best friend. He doesn't fit any of what I just said. The realization has me finally facing what I have to do when we get home.

When I suddenly get quiet, Kyle's piercing gaze hits mine. "What? Do you not?"

"I don't think Rafe thinks of me that way. I thought things would blossom if we spent more time together, but it doesn't feel serious to me."

Kyle releases a breath he seems to have been holding. "Well, he's an idiot if he doesn't hold on to you for dear life."

My eyes flick over his face, trying to read his thoughts. My phone buzzes at that moment, drawing my attention.

"Speak of the devil," Kyle comments, sitting up.

"It's not him."

Kyle looks at me suspiciously. "Who else would be texting you in the middle of the night?"

"My ex," I admit.

Kyle bristles at my words. "Why?"

"He won't leave me alone."

"Block him."

"I can't."

Kyle's eyes narrow, like he's trying to read my face.

My shoulders slump, and I admit the one secret that casts a dark shadow over my life. "He has pictures of me."

"What kinds of pictures?" Kyle pops his knuckles as he asks, his fist closing tight.

I give him a look that says, *you know very well what kind.* "The kind I don't want getting out. They're from when we were dating. Like an idiot, I let him take naked pictures of me."

"And he won't delete them?"

"Actually worse," I admit. "He's threatening to post them if I don't send him money."

"What?" Kyle's jaw clenches with anger. "Where does this asshole live?"

"Burbank."

"What does he do for a living?"

I frown at the strange question. "He has an auto repair shop."

"Really? What's his name?"

"Jerry. Why?"

"What's his shop called?"

"Jerry's Auto Repair. Why?"

He shakes his head. "No reason. I know a few auto places. Never heard of Jerry's."

His voice sounds nonchalant, but there's a tightness in his jaw. He doesn't say anything else, but I can tell he's fuming. I sit up and nudge his shoulder, trying to change the mood. "That band was pretty good, huh?"

"Yeah."

"Don't think I didn't see you dancing by the end of it," I tease.

"I'll never admit to it," he jokes back.

And just like that, the tension dissipates, and the mood lightens.

We continue to talk about everything from our childhoods to our favorite ice cream flavors until the sun peaks over the horizon, casting clouds in pink, gold, and purples.

"That's beautiful," I whisper.

"It sure is. Maybe all those clouds will give us a cool day today."

"Oh, that'd be nice."

"Come on." Kyle rises and pulls me to my feet. "We need to get some shuteye before the lunch rush."

"Not serving breakfast?" I ask as his warm hand engulfs mine, holding long after I'm standing.

"Nah. I didn't want to tackle too many things. Besides, we can only store so much food."

"Well, better for us. Now we can sleep in."

He grins and finally releases my hand.

Once we're in the camper, I slip into the bathroom to change into pajamas and brush my teeth.

When I emerge, the beds have been pulled out and made up, and Kyle has donned a pair of athletic shorts and is peeling his shirt over his head. His abs ripple, and I have to remind myself to close my mouth.

I quickly climb into bed before he can notice me gawking. I keep my back turned to him. "Goodnight," I call, not daring to look at his sexy body again.

I try to clear my head to rest, but it's hard knowing a sexy man is so close to me I could reach out and touch him. I wonder if I'll get any sleep at all.

CHAPTER SEVENTEEN

Sutton—

When I finally wake, it's to the pitter patter of rain on the camper roof. I rise, yawning, and immediately note Kyle's empty bed. My eyes shift to the bathroom, but that too is empty.

Grabbing my phone, I realize it's late afternoon. *Shit.* He must have let me sleep in. That's sweet, but I am here to work. He should have woken me up.

I rush to get ready, throw my hair into a messy bun, then dash out the door.

I'm immediately greeted by a long line, winding its way down the pathway.

As I enter, Kyle calls over his shoulder. "How'd you sleep?"

"Are you serious? How can you be so calm when you're elbows deep in orders?"

"Meh." He shrugs. "These people have all been real understanding with the fact that I was a one man show."

"Sorry," I moan as I rush over to take orders.

"I wasn't criticizing you. I was just letting you know everything's good."

I nod, but still feel a pang of guilt.

It takes nearly two hours to get our heads above water.

"Gosh, it's really coming down." I lean out the order window and watch the festival goers trudge through the mud, holding jackets over their heads. "I thought the desert didn't get rain."

"I didn't think we'd get any, either. Thank God Green gave me the plywood. It's the only thing keeping us from being stuck."

We serve a few more stragglers, and then Kyle closes for our own lunch break.

"Want to just eat some chicken chili?" He gestures to the large pot.

"It seems like the perfect meal for a rainy day."

"Yeah, everyone seems to think that. But I'm not complaining." He grins.

I climb from the truck and immediately slip, landing on my ass in a pile of mud.

"Sutton, are you okay?" Kyle jumps down next to me, laughing.

"I'm not hurt, if that's what you're asking," I grumble at the mud covering my legs and shorts.

"Good, then I don't feel as bad about laughing."

I narrow my eyes. "This isn't funny."

"You're right." He sobers. "It's fucking hilarious." He rears his head back and belly laughs.

"You're an ass. At least help me up."

"Okay, okay." He reaches down to pull me up, but instead, I give him a good yank, and he falls flat into the mud next to me.

"Who's laughing now?" I squeal over my own laughter.

"Did you really just start a mud fight with me?" He cocks an eyebrow, then lifts a handful of mud and tosses it at the side of my head.

"Not my hair!" I cry out, but I'm still laughing.

We proceed to chuck mud back and forth at each other until a group walking by decides to join in. Soon, all around us, mud is flying, and we're both covered head to toe in it.

"Look what you started," I chastise.

"Me?" He holds a hand to his chest. "Woman, *you* started this."

Someone runs behind me, trying to dodge a mud pie. They turn and ram into me, pushing me into Kyle's arms. My hands slam against his chest, and he grabs ahold of my hips to steady us. Our laughter trails off as we stare into each other's eyes.

"Um, we should go clean up," I whisper, "before the dinner rush."

Kyle steps back, and the spell is broken. "Yeah."

We make our way into the RV.

"Oh shit, we're tracking mud everywhere." Kyle stops in the doorway. "Green is going to kill me if we get mud on anything." He steps a little farther in and grabs my duffel bag, sliding it toward the bathroom. "You take a shower first. I'll try my best to clean up at the sink until you're out."

I slip my muddy shoes off, and move to the shower. When I see myself in the mirror, I burst out laughing again. "You didn't say I looked this bad," I shout through the door.

"I didn't want to hurt your ego," he quips.

It takes a good long while before I get all the caked-in mud out of my hair. Thankfully, I find a roll of trash bags under the sink. I unroll one and throw my muddy clothes inside.

When I emerge from the bathroom, I immediately come to a halt. Kyle is standing at the sink in nothing but his boxer briefs, and they don't leave much to the imagination.

"Your... um, y-your turn." I stumble over my words, my cheeks heating with embarrassment.

"Great."

I towel my hair, so he doesn't see my blush as he moves past me.

I dig through the cabinets and find two clear, disposable rain ponchos. Slipping one over my head, I leave the other on the counter with a note. By the time he's finished, I'm in the food truck.

The door opens, and he jumps up, wearing his own poncho.

"There you are."

"I thought it was safer to just eat in here." I smile from where I sit crisscross on the floor.

He pulls off his wet poncho and makes his own bowl, then joins me.

When we finish, the rain has come to a drizzle, but the clouds still loom overhead.

The slow in rain means for a big night in sales. But the rain only holds off for a few hours before it is like a monsoon. We manage to make it to the camper and decide to stay in tonight.

I'm exhausted and fall into a deep sleep.

The next morning, the ground is saturated, and there is quite a bit of standing water. Thankfully, people have to eat, even if the music acts can't carry on, so Kyle is still making a killing.

On the last night, it's clear there is a problem. Some cars have attempted to leave, but immediately find they're stuck. A few make it out of the parking lot, only to get stuck a few feet down the road. No one's getting out anytime soon, and no one's going to get to us, either.

"Looks like we're officially stranded," Kyle announces as he climbs into the camper.

"How long do you think?"

"Probably a couple more days. The ground's got to dry out. Thankfully, it's stopped raining."

"Are we going to keep selling food, then?"

"Until we run out."

I nod. "All right. I better call Rafe."

"Yeah, I need to call the club."

We make another killing at lunch and have just opened for dinner.

"The card says declined." I hand it to the man at the window.

"My rent must have come out. Um…" The guy nervously searches through his wallet.

"Do you have another card?"

"No, I only brought the one. Let me see if I can find some cash." He fidgets through his pockets.

Kyle pushes the food forward. "Don't worry about it."

"Thanks, man." Relief floods his face.

He starts to turn, but Kyle stops him.

"If you need food, you come back here. I've got you. No need for you to go hungry because we all got stuck in a surprise monsoon."

The man chuckles timidly, and his cheeks flush, but he nods.

"Well, aren't you Mr. Charity?" I tease.

"Not really. I just know a lot of hardworking people live on a tight budget, and unexpected expenses can put them in a hardship. I'm not going to be the one to do that to someone because they're hungry and by no fault of their own, they got stuck here."

"Look over there." I point to two other food trucks. "They've doubled their pricing."

"What assholes. I'm not going to take advantage of the situation. At this point, it's about looking out for each other."

I grab his shoulder. He shrugs out of my touch, but turns to look at me.

I hold my hands awkwardly in front of me. "That's really kind of you. You're a good man."

"Thanks," he mumbles. Then he turns to the grill.

More and more people have trouble paying, and eventually Kyle tells me to stop charging. He puts a sign up that says *Venmo if you can. Don't worry if you can't. No one is going to ask for money here.*

When he sees me watching him tape it up, he shrugs. "No need to embarrass people who can't pay."

My smile brightens. Who'd have thought the big bad biker was really a big ol' teddy bear?

After closing shop on our third night stuck, I decide to stretch my legs.

"I'm going to head for a walk. I'll be back in about twenty minutes."

"Okay, see you soon," he calls from where he's watching a football game on his phone.

I walk past all the regular shops, waving at a few. I turn and walk along the camps. It's crazy to see so many tents littering the ground. Man, am I glad we didn't have to camp in this muck. Then I turn and make my way toward the stages. It's weird with them still standing, but no equipment. I walk behind one, curious what's back there, and immediately regret the decision.

I didn't notice the guy trailing behind me.

"What's a pretty thing like you doing over here?" a tall, lanky man purrs.

"Oh, I was just looking." I'm not sure if he's one of the crew tasked with breaking down the stages once everything dries out. I go to move around him, but he sidesteps in front of me.

"No need to run off." He smiles, but it doesn't reach his eyes.

"I need to get back to my boss. He'll be looking for me."

"Really?" He chuckles and brushes a strand of my hair between his fingers.

"Don't touch me," I growl, and bat his hand away.

"You're a feisty one. I was promised a concert series, and instead, I've been lying on the cold, damp ground. I think I deserve something soft and warm." He takes a step toward me.

"I'll scream." But I barely get the words out when he moves like lightning and clamps his clammy hand on top of my mouth, pushing me against the rear of the stage.

I try to bite him, but he's holding my mouth so tightly, I can't get it open.

He rips at my shirt, tearing the sleeve open and revealing my lace bra underneath.

"Oh yeah, you're going to be a real treat." His hot breath rushes in my ear.

He squeezes my breast tightly enough I let out a muffled cry, which seems to excite him. His hand trails down my stomach, and I thrash to get out of his grasp, tears filling my eyes.

He knocks me to the ground and puts his weight on top of me, effectively pinning me.

I manage to get one scream out before he covers my mouth again.

He fumbles with the buttons on my shorts when suddenly, he's thrown from me.

I scramble backward and get my feet under me.

Kyle looms over the man.

He's come for me. Thank God.

His eyes sweep over me, drifting to my torn shirt, and fury darkens his eyes.

"Sorry, man, is she yours?" The man staggers to his own feet and walks backward with his hands up. "We were just having a little fun, weren't we, doll?"

Kyle charges him, throwing a punch that knocks him to the ground. He climbs on top of the guy and pounds into his face until each hit splatters blood, and a sickening crunching sound carries to me.

"Kyle, stop!" I cry, fearful he's going to kill the man. I don't want that on my conscience.

He finally stops, leaving the man a bloody heap, and then walks over to me. "Are you okay?"

"Yes, just scared."

"I've got you, baby." He holds my face between his hands. "I got you."

The tears start to flow, and he pulls me in for a hug. I clutch at him, burrowing into his warm neck.

"Let's get out of here before somebody comes upon us," he whispers against my temple. "I'd rather not have to explain anything to the police."

I dare a peek at the crumpled man on the ground. He's covered in blood, and I'm not sure he's breathing.

As we walk back, fear turns to anger. He may have just killed a man.

"What were you thinking, Kyle?" I whirl at him once we're back in the RV, and he slams the door behind him. "Why did you lose your shit like that? You might have killed him."

"Why did I lose my shit? Do you honestly not know?"

He stalks across the RV, and I retreat until my back is against the wall. His forearm rests above my head, and his other hand grips my hip. His thumb traces small circles on my bare midriff. I don't even think he notices, but I feel every sensation tingling through my body.

"Why I never wanted you working with me? Why I can't stand to be close to you? Because the sweet smell of your hair, like apples and honey, drives me to distraction. Your skin brushing against me singes, because I can feel the velvety softness sending my mind down dark, erotic tunnels I should never venture. I spend every waking moment wanting you to be with me."

My cheeks flush, and my stomach ties in knots. Everything inside me begs for his touch, but knowing I can't do that to Rafe.

Kyle leans closer, until he's only a breath away. "You're my brother's girl. So, I can't do the things I want to do. I can't touch you. Instead, I spend day after day in torture, wanting what I can't have."

"Can't have... or are too afraid to go after?" I challenge, my breath panting from my chest.

He pushes himself from the wall. It feels like a bucket of ice water has been dumped on me, and the greater the distance he puts between us, the colder and emptier I feel.

He shoves the door open and steps down from the truck, turning back. "I think the words you were forgetting were thank you." Then he slams the door.

"Thank you," I whisper to no one.

CHAPTER EIGHTEEN

Sutton—

Finally, the ground is dry enough that people are beginning to leave.

A man approaches our window, and Kyle dips his head. "Can I help you, sir?"

"If you're goin', now's your chance. Word is that people are getting through. They say another storm is moving in tomorrow."

Kyle glances at the sky. "Thanks, man."

He nods and moves away.

Kyle's eyes shift to me. "Guess we should pack it up."

I look at the soft ground. "You sure?"

"I don't want to risk staying. We could get stuck for a week and run out of food. I need to make sure you get home safe."

Because everything between us is awkward now? Is that why he's in a hurry to leave? He's barely spoken to me since the other night. I feel like I've ruined everything.

My shoulders slump. "You're right."

He stares at me for a moment, like there's something more he wants to say, but in the end, he just turns to the grill and starts cleaning it.

I wash utensils and pack them up. It takes us two hours, and the line leading out the only road in is getting long as more and more people decide to try getting out. Some of the other food trucks are sunk in the mud up to their wheel wells.

"Those poor people," I murmur, watching out the window.

Kyle nods. "That stuff's probably like cement by now. I'm glad Green made me bring the plywood."

"What will happen to them?"

"I don't know, Sutton. Maybe they'll send in the National Guard to get them out. I'm sure the promotors have contacted someone. Maybe they'll bring in military helicopters with food. By now, surely this disaster has made the news."

"I suppose you're right."

Within an hour, we're packed and rolling slowly in the long line of RVs, mini-vans, and pickup trucks.

I stare out the window and think about our time here. I can't work with Kyle anymore. He's right. It'll be too hard. And I can't pull apart two brothers who've been so close their entire lives. I know what I've got to do when we get home.

"You okay?"

"Yes. So, your food was a real hit, Kyle. How much did you make?"

"With the food I gave away at the end, I'll be lucky if I break even."

Melancholy washes over me. "So, it was all for nothing?"

"Don't say that. We tried our best. There will be other festivals. I'll make do." He watches me. "Hey."

I turn to meet his eyes.

"You're always the positive one. Don't go getting depressed on me now."

I look out the window.

"Sutton?"

"Yes?"

"You okay?"

I nod.

"I mean about that guy. He tried to hurt you. I don't mean to sound like you don't have a right to be depressed or sad or pissed off."

"I'm fine. And thanks for what you did. I should have said it right away."

He shakes his head. "This isn't about me. I was wrong to say that to you. I was being an ass."

"No, you weren't." I pluck at a thread on the hem of my shirt. "I just wish this had been a success for you. I hate you lost money."

"Well, get to work, marketing manager. Post some of those pictures of the lines we had before the storm hit." He shrugs. "And maybe some of those after."

He's right. I have pictures. Lots of pictures. I even managed to take a couple of the line of wet and muddy people, waiting in the rain for a free hot meal.

I pull my phone out and tap a post, picking just the right photo. It's one I took from the vantage point of the back of the line, showing the truck and the sign Kyle had written.

Maybe it'll help.

"Sutton?"

"Yes?"

"I feel really guilty about what happened. I should have protected you. I should have taken better care of you. I never should have let you go walking alone."

"Don't," I snap. "You can be sorry about what happened to me, but don't you dare take on the guilt or responsibility for what that man did."

His eyes shift to the road. "Is that what I do?"

"You did it with Rafe, didn't you? I mean, you never told me everything, but—"

"He was shot, and I wasn't there for him. I let him go out in that alley alone."

"I'm sure Rafe does a lot of dangerous stuff for the MC. You both do."

"I guess."

"If Cole gave you an order, you'd do it." I can see by the way he shifts in his seat and sucks in a breath, that my words are getting to him. But he needs to face this and realize the truth, or he and Rafe will never have the relationship they had before the night of the shooting.

"It took Rafe a long time to recover," Kyle whispers. "A *long* time. You'd maybe never know it now, but he had a rocky road of physical therapy. He had to relearn how to walk, how to talk. It was bad."

"I hate that for him."

"He ever tell you any of this?"

"No."

Kyle stares out the windshield. "Maybe he doesn't like to talk about it. Sometimes, I'm not even sure what he remembers. He lost a lot of memories."

"It's sad, but I try not to be sad for him. I know the last thing he wants is pity."

"Yeah."

"It costs a lot to face the truth. You can be sorry about something and not take on the guilt and responsibility for it," I murmur.

We spend most of the rest of the trip in silence. Eventually, I doze off. When I wake, we're on I5.

Kyle stops to get gas, and I can see the exhaustion on his face.

"Let me drive," I offer.

"It's a big RV pulling a big trailer, Sutton. You have any experience?"

"No, I guess not."

"I'll be fine. I just need some coffee." He hangs the nozzle on the gas pump. "You want anything?"

I shake my head.

Ten minutes later, we're back on the road.

It's almost midnight when we get home. Kyle drives me to Rafe's house, and idles in the street, and calls his brother.

"Get your ass up, and come get your woman, loser," Kyle teases.

A minute later, Rafe strolls down the drive in just a pair of jeans.

"Are you working tomorrow?" I ask.

"Nah. Gonna sleep in."

I pull on the door handle.

"Thanks for everything, Sutton," Kyle says.

"You're welcome." I stare at him a long moment, then walk around the front of the RV to meet Rafe.

He hugs me and waves to his brother. The RV and trailer, still covered in dried mud, pull away, and I watch the taillights disappear.

CHAPTER NINETEEN

Kyle—

The smell of the coffee in my mug hits my nose as I lean against my kitchen counter and pull up Jerry's Auto Repair in Burbank. It's open until 5:30pm. Scanning, I find a photo of the owner. Jerry's smiling face stares back at me. "Smile, motherfucker. Soon you're not going to have any front teeth left. You'll be drinking through a straw for a long fucking time."

I take a sip of coffee and map it out on my app. Five hours. That's a haul, but this is a trip I don't mind making. The clock on the wall says quarter to noon, and I need to get going if I plan to make it before closing time.

Dumping the dregs of my coffee in the sink, I grab my cut off the back of the chair and head out to my Harley just as TJ pulls in my drive.

Shit.

He shuts his bike off, noticing I'm checking my saddlebags.

"Where are you headed?"

"Got somewhere I've got to be," I say without really answering.

"I'll ride along."

"Not this time." I swing my leg over the seat and lift my bike off the kickstand.

"Why not? What's so secretive?"

"You don't need to be involved in this, TJ."

He tilts his head. "You're not going to Rafe's place, are you?"

I huff a laugh. "Why? What do you think I'm gonna do?"

"I don't know, but you've got that 'I'm going to beat the shit out of someone' look in your eye."

"And it's gotta be Rafe?"

"No, but you've seemed a little…" He trails off.

"A little what?"

He shrugs. "Like you've lost patience with him."

"Maybe I have, but that's not what this is about. I've got to go."

"When will you be back?"

"By eleven."

"Come have a beer with me at the clubhouse when you get back."

I nod and fire my bike up, drop it in gear, and hit the throttle, roaring out of the drive and down the street. Checking my side mirror, I see TJ making a call.

He better not try to follow me. This is my deal, not the club's.

The ride is monotonous, and I spend most of it on autopilot, trying not to dwell on what I'm about to do. Roughing people up isn't my favorite part of the club, but I'm not doing it for the club. I'm doing it for Sutton, and I'm going to enjoy this one. I don't think Cole will mind that I do it wearing my cut. He's always been a staunch protector of women—never one to stand by and let anyone disrespect them, even the dancers down at Sonny's Gentleman's Club.

Finally, I hit Burbank and find Victory Blvd. It's a four-lane road lined with orange trees and small, one level businesses. I pass a bowling alley, a couple of cash advance franchises, and a bail bonds place.

The orange trees are in blossom, and it smells like someone dumped a bottle of perfume on the town.

I come to the intersection of Providencia and spot the place I'm looking for on the left-hand corner. It's a small cement block building with two double-bays in an area lined with a bunch of other collision centers, body shops, and auto repair places.

I stop at the light and check the time. Ten minutes until they close for the night.

When the light turns green, I make a left down the side street and find an alley behind the building. Perfect. I roll in and park. Reaching inside my cut, I grab my phone and check his photo again, so I don't make a mistake. I climb from my bike, stretch, and walk to the corner. There's a bus stop and I lean against a lamppost to light up a cigarette, like I'm waiting for a bus.

Blowing smoke toward the sky, it doesn't take me long to spot Jerry. He's got slicked back dark hair and rolled up short sleeves, like he thinks he's James Dean or something. He looks like the tough guy who folds the moment a man worth his salt challenges him—the guy who only throws his weight around with women and those weaker than him. I've seen his kind a million times in this MC life.

Any time the club walks into a bar, there's always some guy thinks he's gonna challenge us. But guys like Jerry usually lose their backbone in the first thirty seconds and head out the back door with their tails between their legs.

Since it's near closing, only one other guy is still there. I smoke another cigarette and stay out of sight around some bushes.

When his last employee goes to his car, I yank my gloves from my back pocket, slip them on, and make my move. Crossing the small parking lot, I stroll nonchalantly into one of the garage bays before Jerry gets the overhead doors pulled down.

"We're closed, sir. Come back in the morning," he says, pulling the chain on the first overhead door. It rumbles into place, the sound echoing through the garage. Somewhere a sound system is playing Johnny Cash's *Ring of Fire*.

"I only need a minute." I glance around, looking for security cameras, but I don't see any.

"Okay," he says, slowing his actions when he sees my cut. "What can I do for you? You got a car that needs repair?"

I yank the chain, slamming the second set of doors down, and now. Jerry backs up a step.

"No, Jerry. I don't have a car."

He frowns. "Do I know you?"

"Nope. I'm here about Sutton."

"Sutton? What about her?" His eyes follow my movements as I pick up a nearby tire iron and walk toward him. He lifts his hands. "I don't want any trouble, mister."

"Too bad. 'Cause trouble just found you." I swing and break his femur, hearing it crunch as he goes down. I'm over him in a second with my arm raised.

Jerry's hands go up in a defensive position. "No, please. Don't kill me."

"I hear you've got pictures of Sutton. Pictures you've been threatening to make public if she doesn't come up with money to buy you off. True? And you better give me the right answer."

"Okay. Yeah, I did." He moans, tears streaming down his face. "Motherfucker, that hurts. I need an ambulance."

"You don't tell me what I want to hear, you're gonna need a coroner and a trip to the morgue."

"I'll tell you whatever you want to know. Please. T-there's money in the drawer." His shaking hand points toward a small office.

"I don't want your fucking money. Where are the pictures?"

"On my phone. They're all on my phone."

"What about your computer? A jump drive? The cloud?"

"No, I swear. Just my phone."

"I find out you're lying to me, they'll never find your body. Do you understand?"

He nods, his teeth gritted against the pain.

"So, one more time, Jerry. Where are they?"

"My phone. Just my phone. I swear it."

I hold out my hand. "Give it to me."

He digs into his pocket and hands it over.

"What's the code?" I ask.

"6969."

I shake my head. What a sophomoric asshole. It unlocks, and I go to his photos. Scrolling, I see he's got naked photos of a lot of different women. I whistle. "You're a regular Romeo, aren't you? Or maybe you're a rapist and serial killer."

"What?"

I punch him in the face again and again until it's pouring blood onto his shirt. "Take your fucking shirt off."

He can't talk at this point. I probably broke his jaw, but he shrugs out of it, ripping the buttons down the front and tossing it to me.

I grab it, squat, and hold it in front of his face. "You see this blood? That's your DNA. You ever do another thing to harm Sutton in any fucking way, the cops are gonna find your shirt and DNA at a horrific murder scene. We clear?"

He nods, barely able to hold his head up.

"You go to the cops, I'll destroy your life." Then I stand, kick him in the nuts, and stroll quietly out to the alley. I don't pass a soul as I leave.

Reaching my bike, I stuff the shirt in my saddlebag, pull out of the alley, and head farther down the side street. I make a big loop through the backstreets until I can find my way to I5 and make the five-hour ride to San Jose.

When I hit town, I ride to the clubhouse. There are only a few bikes parked out front. I recognize all of them and know immediately who's inside. TJ, Marcus, and Billy.

Climbing from my bike, I stretch, my muscles aching from the ten-plus hours I've spent in the saddle today. The music is low background noise, and I see the guys sitting at the bar. They turn when I walk in.

TJ motions to the prospect behind the bar, and the kid brings me an ice-cold long neck. I press it to my forehead, letting the coolness sink into my skin.

"You okay?" TJ asks.

"Yeah." Twisting the cap off, I down a big portion.

"You take care of whatever it was you went to take care of?" TJ asks, obviously fishing for an explanation.

"Yep." The one-word answer is all I give him.

"That all you're gonna tell us?" Billy asks.

I lift a brow to TJ. "You've been busy, I see."

"I was worried about you, man." His eyes drop to my hand on the bottle, and he frowns.

I glance down to see my swollen knuckles.

"Brother, you been in a fistfight?" he asks.

"Just had some business to take care of. I took care of it. End of story."

"Why you gotta be such a closed-up motherfucker?" TJ snaps.

"Because it's my business."

His eyes narrow. "This got anything to do with Sutton?"

My eyes flare when he hits the nail on the head. I tip my bottle up.

"Jesus, it's like trying to pry the nuclear codes from you. We're your brothers. No secrets, remember?"

"Bullshit. You don't get to know about my private life," I snap.

Billy chuckles. "You don't have a private life, Kyle. We all know it."

TJ studies me for a few seconds, then presses again. "And this wasn't about Rafe?"

"Nope."

"Just spill, bro," Marcus huffs. "You know he's not gonna let it go. TJ's like a dog with a bone when he thinks he's on to something."

I lean on the bar, my shoulders tight. "Just doin' Rafe's job."

"Rafe's job?" Billy asks. "What do you mean?"

"I mean, I stepped up and took care of a problem Rafe should have dealt with."

"Yeah? What's that?"

I tip my bottle up again, finishing and pushing it forward for another. The prospect hurries over with a replacement, snatching away the empty.

"Kyle? Come on. Spill," TJ presses. "Ain't nothin' you can't tell us."

I consider his words and know they're true. If I needed a body buried, they'd grab a shovel. "There's an ex-boyfriend hustling Sutton. I took care of it."

"Hustling her how?" Billy asks.

"Blackmailing her. Seems he had some nude shots he'd taken of her when they were dating."

"No shit?" Marcus mutters. "What'd you do?"

"I went and delivered a message. Then I confiscated his phone."

"And?" TJ asks.

"And he's gonna be drinking through a straw and using crutches for a long while."

"Dude," TJ says, grinning.

"We could have helped you," Billy offers.

"Nope. Like I said, this was my responsibility."

"Actually, it was Rafe's responsibility. He know about this guy?" TJ asks.

I shake my head. "I don't know if Sutton told him."

"But she told you?" Marcus asks.

"Yeah, she told me. What of it?" I snap.

He holds his palms up. "Whoa. Chill out, man."

"Rafe should have been the one to do that," TJ says.

"Yeah, he should have. Guess he didn't care enough." I sound bitter, even to my own ears.

"But you don't know if she told him, Kyle. You just said as much. He deserves the benefit of the doubt until you know," Marcus says quietly.

He's right. "Where is he?"

"It was his turn staking out Joselyn Silver, making sure she didn't go after Carlo Bianchi," Billy explains. "He called this afternoon and said she was in her Mercedes headed south on 15. Cole told him to stay on her. She could have been headed to LA. We didn't know. When she picked up Highway 58 east toward Bakersfield, Cole figured she had to be going to Vegas. He and the other originals went to head her off."

"She was almost to Vegas when they caught up with her. They should be home tomorrow."

I polish off my second beer and push from the bar. "I'm tired. I'll see you boys tomorrow."

Heading to my bike, I text Sutton.

ME: JUST HEARD RAFE WAS CALLED OUT OF TOWN ON MC BUSINESS. JUST WANTED TO CHECK IN ON YOU AND MAKE SURE YOU'RE OKAY.
SUTTON: I'M FINE. THANKS.
ME: IF YOU NEED ANYTHING, I'M HERE.
SUTTON: I'M GOOD. THANKS.
ME: TOMORROW I'M GONNA OPEN UP FOR

LUNCH RUSH DOWN BY THE FARMER'S MARKET. IF YOU WANT TO WORK, I CAN SWING BY AND PICK YOU UP

SUTTON: SURE. I'LL WORK.

ME: GREAT. SEE YOU AT TEN

SUTTON: OK. GOODNIGHT

ME: SLEEP TIGHT

CHAPTER TWENTY

Sutton—

I hear Kyle's pickup truck and glance out the window. By the time I reach him, he's at the passenger side to hold the door for me.

My eyes scan over the trailer. "Looks like you've been busy. All the mud's gone."

"It was a mess, wasn't it? I spent an hour scrubbing down the RV before I returned it to Green."

"I should have helped you," I say.

"Nah. I took it to the clubhouse and had the prospects help me."

"Oh." I slip inside, and he goes around and gets behind the wheel. The truck shifts with his weight. It smells like his soap, and I breathe deep, stealing any bit of him I can get.

I've thought a lot about things, and I know things can't go on the way they have. I have feelings for Rafe, but I've come to realize they'll never be the kind of feelings that are made to last a lifetime—the kind someone uses to build a lifelong relationship.

I have those feelings for Kyle, and that makes this situation impossible. I can't come between two brothers who are as close as these two men are.

I'll have to decide how to end things with Rafe in a way that doesn't leave him blaming or hating Kyle. Though, I'm not even sure how strongly Rafe would react.

In the meantime, I can't leave Kyle hanging with no help at the food truck, even though it's becoming an increasingly unbearable situation to be working in such close quarters. Being near him drives me wild, and it's crazy to put myself or both of us through this absolute torment.

We set up and work the lunch rush.

At one point, a van for the local news station pulls up, and a cameraman climbs out. Behind him, I recognize one of the local newscasters. Her name is Amy, and she does a fluff spot called About Town with Amy.

I peer out the window. "I wonder what Channel Five is doing here."

Kyle dips his head. "No clue."

He gets back to making food, and Amy approaches the truck.

I smile and wave. "Hi, Amy. What can we get you?"

"Hi, there. I was looking for Kyle." She cranes to peer around me.

"Oh, sure." I glance over at him. "She wants to talk to you."

He frowns, busy with what he's doing. "Who does?"

"The lady from Channel Five. Amy Armstrong."

His eyes shift to me, then dart to the window. "She does?" He walks over and leans down. "I'm Kyle. What can I do for you?"

"Could I speak with you for a couple of minutes?"

"I'm kind of busy."

"I promise it won't take long."

He drags in a breath.

"Go," I tell him. "I've got this. Besides, it might mean some publicity for us."

"Maybe you should talk to her. You're better than me at this stuff."

"It's *your* truck. Go. Hurry."

He unties his apron and tosses it. "Fine. I hate this stuff, you know."

I make a face, and he finally puts a grin on, then steps from the trailer.

About twenty minutes later, he comes back in, and we finish the line.

"Thanks for covering for me," he says with a strange look on his face.

"What's wrong?" I ask.

"Nothing. News about the festival travels fast, I guess. They had heard reports about how I gave away food to those in need." He suddenly cocks his head. "Did you post about that?"

"Who me?" I put a hand to my chest. "I may have posted a shot of the line waiting in the rain and mud."

"She must have seen it. Apparently, it's spread all over the internet. She wanted to interview me about the situation up there from my perspective."

"That's great."

"She said they're always on the lookout for feel-good stories to share, and what I'd done was encouraging and uplifting for a lot of people. It'll be on the air tomorrow night."

"Wow. This is great news. Aren't you happy?"

"I guess."

"Maybe it'll help business."

"I hope so. I need to make up the money I lost at the festival."

Just then, TJ walks to the window. "Did you say you lost money?"

"Hey, brother. Yeah. I came out in the negative."

"Well, that sucks."

The line has died down, and I see Gigi behind TJ. I wave to her, and Kyle notices.

"Why don't you go take a break?" He shoves a container of freshly made onion rings at me. "Here. Go have a chat."

I'm not sure if he's trying to get rid of me so he can talk MC stuff with TJ, so I accept them. As I step out of the truck, I hear TJ ask him a question.

"You tell her about yesterday?"

I turn around, and Kyle stares at me like a deer caught in the headlights.

"What about yesterday?"

"Nothing," Kyle snaps.

TJ sticks his grinning face in the window. "He took care of that slime ball for you. The one with the photos."

My eyes widen, and Kyle throws a spatula across the grill. "You need to learn to keep your mouth shut, asshole."

TJ grins. "I knew you'd keep it to yourself. She deserves to know."

"What did you do, Kyle?"

Again TJ answers for him. "He took a ride to his garage and beat the shit out of him."

I put my fingertips to my mouth. "Oh, my God. Did you really?"

He won't look or answer me.

"Kyle…"

"Okay, yeah. I did. But you weren't supposed to know about it."

"Way I heard it, he broke the dude's leg," TJ says, still volunteering information and making Kyle glare at him.

"Shut the fuck up, brother."

I stare at Kyle until he turns to me. "Thank you," I mouth.

He gets fidgety, rearranging things. "It was nothing. He got what he deserved."

"It wasn't nothing to me," I reply.

"Go take that break," he growls.

I bite away a smile, climb out of the truck, and walk with Gigi to a nearby table.

She heard everything and studies me with a grin.

"Wow. He really stepped up for you, huh?"

I stare at the truck. "I've been thinking of quitting."

"What? Why?"

"Because I can't do this anymore. I'm starting to have feelings for him."

"Oh," Gigi whispers and tilts her head. "That is a dilemma." She nabs an onion ring and munches on it. "I hear the club will be back soon. TJ thought they'd hit town anytime now."

My shoulders slump.

"That's not exactly the reaction of a girl excited her man is coming home."

"I know. It's horrible, isn't it? I'm horrible."

She reaches across the table. "You're not horrible."

TJ wanders over and snatches an onion ring, his eyes shifting from me to Gigi. "You ready to go?"

I surge to my feet. "I've got to get back to work."

"Sutton, wait," I hear Gigi say, but I'm already fast walking to the trailer. There's another line.

I climb inside and barely look at Kyle. He seems uncomfortable now that I know what he did for me. I still can't believe he rode to Burbank just to put Jerry in his place. No man has ever done that for me. I don't know if Rafe would have done the same. I never told him. Maybe because I was afraid he wouldn't care enough to do anything, and I didn't want to face that.

I slice more onions to batter and put in the fryer.

Kyle glances over his shoulder. "Sorry I didn't tell you about Jerry."

I slip and slice my finger, cursing and dropping the knife.

"You okay?" Kyle's at my side in an instance.

The cut is deep, and blood is pouring out.

He responds quickly, grabbing a bunch of napkins and pressing it to my hand. "Put pressure on it." Then he dashes to the back door. "TJ!"

He catches them right before TJ climbs in his truck with Gigi.

Kyle motions him over, and they both come running.

The next thing I know, they're herding me toward their truck to take me to the emergency room, and Kyle is at my side.

"I've got to shut the food truck down, then I'll be right behind you, okay?"

"That's not necessary," I protest, but he won't hear it. His eyes latch onto TJ's. "Hurry up, brother. It's bleeding bad."

"I got her, Kyle. Don't worry."

Then TJ is pulling away, and Kyle stands at the curb, watching us.

We get to the hospital, and I'm rushed into the second curtained cubicle. A nurse checks me and wraps a clean bandage around my wound.

"The doctor will be in to see you shortly."

"Will she need stitches?" Gigi asks.

"Possibly," the nurse says, being non-committal. She leaves us, and Gigi squeezes my uninjured hand.

"Are you doing okay?"

"I'm fine. It's just throbbing."

She grins. "Maybe they'll give you something good for the pain."

That gets a smile out of me.

"Can I ask you something?" she says.

"Sure."

"Every time I see you and Kyle together, I can't help feeling that it's you two who should have ended up together. Not you and Rafe."

"Do you want to know the truth? It was Kyle who first attracted my attention. But then Rafe made a move, and Kyle just backed off."

"I wonder why he stepped aside."

"I guess I was easy to give up."

"You have no idea how untrue that is," a deep voice says.

I jerk my head and see Kyle standing there.

Gigi's gaze shifts between us. "I, um, think I'll go get a coffee. Want anything? No? Okay."

She steps out.

Kyle moves forward, gesturing to my hand. "How is it?"

"The doctor should be in soon. The nurse thought I might need stitches."

"I'm sorry about that. Guess you can claim workman's comp."

"I'm not going to do that, Kyle."

"Rafe's on his way. They just hit town. I told him to meet us here."

"Oh. Thanks."

"Sorry it took so long for me to get here. It took me a few minutes to unhitch my pickup from the food trailer."

"You could have stayed and worked. You didn't have to come."

"Yeah, I did." Kyle stands there, a ballcap in his hand, squeezing it and bending the brim. He looks like he wants to say something, but before he can get the nerve, the doctor comes in.

"I'm Dr. Kendall. Let's have a look at that hand."

Before I know it, he and a nurse have crowded Kyle, and I see him step outside the curtain. The Doctor examines me, then prepares a hypodermic needle.

"This will pinch, but it'll numb the pain."

And then he cleans my wound and put two stitches in. Afterward, it doesn't take him long to bandage me up.

I hear a scuffle and raised voices in the outer room. The doctor and nurse look at each other but keep going. Once they're finished and step out, Gigi slides back in.

"They're getting the paperwork to release me," I say, then hold my hand up. "Two stitches."

She nods but doesn't smile.

"What's wrong?" I frown. "What was that commotion?"

"Rafe and Kyle got into it."

"What do you mean?" Fear flashes through me.

"Rafe was pissed you got hurt, and he was also pissed you two were out of town for so long. He acted like Kyle did it on purpose."

"That's absurd," I hiss.

"I know. Kyle tried to tell him that."

I roll my eyes. "Men can be so sophomoric."

"Yeah, they can." She glances nervously toward the hall.

"What is it?"

She sighs. "There's more."

"What?"

"Rafe challenged Kyle to a cage fight."

My brows lift. "Did you say cage fight?"

"Yeah. There's an MMA cage in the back part of the clubhouse. They hold fights about once a month."

"You're kidding."

"Nope."

"Why does Rafe want to fight Kyle?"

She shrugs. "I think it's over you."

"That's insane." I shake my head. "I never meant to come between them." My eyes glaze, and Gigi puts an arm around my shoulders.

"Don't cry." She squeezes me. "Maybe this is what they need."

"To fight? That's crazy."

"This has been building for a long time… maybe before you came. I think it all has to do with Rafe's injury."

"Rafe takes advantage of Kyle. Is that what you mean? Even I see it."

"Maybe a good brawl will get it all out in the open."

CHAPTER TWENTY-ONE

Kyle—

My father strolls over as I wrap my hand.

"What the hell did you do?" he snaps.

"Nothing." I'm standing in the room the club uses as a dressing room. I'm already stripped to just my long, black, kickboxing shorts, my chest and feet bare.

He knocks my hands aside and wraps them like a pro. "I don't like this."

"Why not? I've seen enough of you guys settle stuff in the cage."

"You and your brother have always been so close. I don't like this—the damn cage, beating the shit out of each other."

"Maybe it's overdue," I say.

"Shit hasn't been right between the two of you for a while. What's that about?"

"Dad—"

"Is it Sutton?"

"What's that supposed to mean?"

"You tell me. Did you and Sutton hookup behind your brother's back?"

"No, Dad."

"You spent all that time together out of town."

"Doesn't mean I fucked her."

"Then what's this about?"

"This has been building for a long time."

He lifts his chin, his eyes narrowing on me. "Since the shooting."

"Yeah, since the shooting."

"You're a good brother, and he knows it. He takes advantage of that, of the fact that you always back down and let him have his way. I should have put a stop to it." He finishes wrapping my hands.

"Well, he wants a fight. He'll get one." I hear the crowd of brothers in the warehouse. "Who are they betting on?"

"Hell, I don't know. I don't care. And you shouldn't either."

I go to open the door, but his voice stops me.

"Son."

I turn back. "Yeah?"

"The MC knows you're the better fighter. But they're all wondering if you'll knuckle under and throw the match."

My jaw tightens.

"If he wins, he has to earn it. Don't go easy on him. Don't punk out and let him win."

I jerk the door open and stalk toward the cage, fire burning in me. Is that what I always do? Let him win. *Well, not fucking tonight, brother.*

I see Rafe in the cage, dancing around and punching the air, getting warmed up.

Hopping up to the mat, I scan the crowd, but there's only one face I'm looking for, and I don't see her. It's crowded and the lights are on the cage, making the crowd dim shadows. I can't help wondering if Sutton is here, if she's going to watch us fight.

Red Dog is referee tonight, and he motions us together to bump fists. "Okay, boys. Defend yourself. I'll enforce the agreed-upon rules of this competition, but you are responsible for your own safety." Then he grins. "And no nut shots."

He moves away, and Green rings the bell, and it's on.

Rafe taunts me with a grin. "You ready to get your clock cleaned, bro?" He sends a scorching blow that knocks me off balance.

I return his grin. "Glad to see you've decided to show up this time." Then I dig down and charge him, holding nothing back.

Sutton—

I stand behind the crowd of cheering men. If the cage wasn't elevated, I wouldn't be able to see. As it is, I can barely see the shoulders and heads of the two men in the cage: Rafe and Kyle, bouncing around and taking jabs and kicks at each other.

The crowd is loud and echoes in the warehouse. I glance around. Melissa and Gigi are watching me.

They must realize I want to be alone, because they don't approach.

I pray it ends quickly and neither gets hurt, but a part of me hopes Kyle doesn't cave to the immense guilt I know he feels—guilt that always makes him let Rafe win.

Not this time, Kyle. Make him earn it.

I can hear the slap of skin on skin, kicks making connections, even though I can't see them. I stand on tip-toe, but I'm not sure I really want to see and pop back down. I chew on a finger, more worried with the sound of each hit that lands.

Green informed me there are three five-minute rounds. There's a digital clock on the wall, the numbers lit in red. The seconds tick down, but it seems like an eternity.

By the third round, they both look tired. Kyle never hits a blow to Rafe's head, and I'm sure it's because he's being careful. All his shots are to the body and legs.

He spins and does a roundhouse kick, hitting Rafe's hip and making him stagger against the cage. The chain links rattle and shake.

I glance at the clock. There's only about three minutes left, and I'm terrified for both of them. I can't bear the thought of them truly hurting each other. I hope this heals the rift that's grown between them.

When the fight is over, I know what I plan to do—sneak out. But I can't possibly do that until I know how this ends. Until I know that these two brothers who have loved each other their entire lives are finally able to work out their issues. I want them to be happy, and I know I can't stay and come between them.

I glance around the crowd who are like a big family, all watching out for each other. I'll miss them. Every single one of them. I can't believe how quickly they've wormed their way into my heart.

I fade into the shadows and find a box to stand on next to an iron I-beam. It gives me a good view.

Rafe looks tired, but Kyle is still fighting strong.

The crowd is cheering, and the sound is deafening, like a Roman coliseum.

Kyle lunges and drives Rafe into the chain link. He gets a hold and takes Rafe to the mat, pinning him. Seconds tick by as the two men grapple, and Kyle gets his brother in a headlock until finally Rafe taps out.

The crowd roars. Green throws his hands in the air, like he just won a bunch of money, and the two brothers break apart.

Red Dog tugs Rafe to his feet, then lifts Kyle's hand in the air in victory.

The crowd roars again.

When I see Rafe is okay, I slip out the door and down the hall to the main clubhouse. Hurrying past the bar, I see a prospect wiping glasses.

"You okay, ma'am?"

I slip out the door and spot Crystal's car idling in the parking lot. I climb into the front seat. "Thanks for coming."

"No problem. Who won?"

"Kyle."

"You sure about this?" she asks.

I nod, and she pulls out.

"My sons are both headstrong, and sometimes they're stubborn as hell. They make mistakes, I won't deny it. But they'd never mean to hurt you, Sutton."

I swivel my head. "It's not me I'm worried about. I can't bear to tear them apart. Things haven't turned out the way I thought they would with Rafe. I thought in time, we'd grow closer, our relationship would deepen. But that just hasn't happened."

"And Kyle? Do you have feelings for him?"

I swallow. "That's why I have to go."

"What if he has feelings for you?"

"Don't you see? It'll always be a thing between them. It won't work."

She drives me to Rafe's, where I pack my bags and leave him a note. Then she takes me to the Diridon Transit Center. I can catch a train to Stockton or a bus to Santa Cruz. I'm not sure which way I'll go yet.

"I hate leaving you like this," Crystal says. "Are you sure you'll be okay?"

"Yes. Thanks for everything."

"Will you at least let them know where you're going?"

"I left Rafe a note," I say.

"I can't help feeling you're making a mistake," she replies, her eyes sad.

"I can't come between them. I don't want to be responsible for that."

"All right. I can respect that." She reaches into her handbag and passes me an envelope. "My number's in there, plus a little cash for the road."

"I can't take that."

"I insist." Then she reaches across and hugs me. "It's never too late to change your mind. You're always welcome."

"Thank you." I slip out of the car and carry my bag into the station. My eyes blur, and I blink away the tears.

CHAPTER TWENTY-TWO

Kyle—

My spatula scrapes across the grill, scooping a patty and flipping it. There's a short line, but nothing I can't handle. The beef sizzles, and I stare. I've been on autopilot since I arrived, my mind on the fight yesterday.

When the third round ended, and Red Dog lifted my arm high in the air, I was exhilarated. I searched the crowd for Sutton, but I never found her.

It felt good to beat Rafe. I wanted to know what she thought of the outcome.

Rafe congratulated me, but then left before we could talk. He'd come up short, and his face was red. I wasn't there to rub it in. He just needed to learn I was no longer going to smooth the bumps in life for him.

I didn't see Sutton leave with him, but so many of the club were gathered around me with back slaps and offers of shots. I missed Rafe slipping out.

Thoughts of Sutton have been on my mind ever since. I was sure she'd at least make eye contact with me across the room, even if she didn't actually congratulate me. I would have understood, but nothing at all? Not even anger?

That's not the Sutton I know.

When she didn't show up today, I texted her, but she didn't reply.

Maybe that's an indication of how angry she is. Perhaps she blames me for the fight or thinks I should have stopped it.

If that's the case, I suppose she's done working for me. I guess I can't blame her. Working for me has put her in an untenable position. It was selfish of me to ask her to work the other day.

I wonder how her hand is doing, and I can't help worrying about her.

Maybe I should text her again. Maybe I should get the guts to call her.

What the fuck are you doing? You know the answer to that. She's not your girl. She's Rafe's. She's off-limits. Completely.

I work hard the rest of the afternoon and finally catch a break right before the dinner rush. Plopping on a stool, I chug a bottle of water.

Out of the corner of my eye, I see the Channel Five news van pull up. Christ, I hope she's not back for another interview. Maybe she's here about some other vendor at the Farmer's Market.

Her camera crew exits the van, and Amy fixes her hair in a compact, then closes her door and rounds the van where she pulls out a long foam board, carrying it like a surfboard under her arm. I can only see the back of it, so I have no clue what kind of stunt she's up to this time. I'm expecting her to walk on past and head inside, but she makes a beeline right for me.

"What now?" I mutter, and stand to lean on the counter, dipping my head low to talk to her through the window. "Amy Armstrong, Channel Five News. Nice to see you again."

"Hi, Kyle. Could you step out here for a moment? I have something for you."

My eyes fall to the big thing she's carrying, puzzled. "Yeah. Sure."

I close the order window, head to the back door and drop to the asphalt, hoping to get this over with before people on the street start gawking.

"What can I do for you, Miss Armstrong?"

She holds up the microphone and pastes a big smile on her face, looking at the cameraman.

"I'm here today with Kyle, the owner of Kyle's food truck. I know many of you remember our story about his kindness during the monsoon out at the Tribe Music Festival last week." Then she turns to me. "Kyle, when our viewers saw your story, we were inundated with calls, asking how they could repay you for your kindness. So, my producer at Channel Five started an account. As of this morning, people from all across the Bay area have donated one-hundred and eighty-seven thousand dollars." She spins the foam board around, and I see it's a giant check.

My mouth drops open. "Is this a joke?"

"No, sir. You've got a lot of fans out there. We even heard from many of those festival attendees whom you helped with your kind generosity. They wanted to help you recoup some of the money you lost. Even some bands kicked in." She stares at me, then turns to the camera. "I think he's speechless, folks."

"I don't know what to say," I mumble, still glancing around, wondering if this is a gag. I cock my head. "Did the club put you up to this?"

She stills, her chin pulling to the side, but keeps the smile pasted on her face, her eyes shifting between me and the camera. "What club?"

"Never mind. I'm just stunned. That's all." I point at the foam check. "Is that thing for real?"

She laughs. "Well, we have some paperwork for you to fill out and the money will be deposited into your account, but this is yours to keep." She passes it to me, and we both grin at the camera for a minute.

She makes a slashing motion with her hand. "Cut. I think we got what we need, Hal."

Hal lowers the camera, and there's a smattering of applause from people gathering on the sidewalk.

"Look, I'm sorry if I didn't give you the reaction you expected. This is a little crazy, you know?" I mumble.

"No problem. You were great."

"This is insane." I stare at the zeros on the check.

"People will surprise you with how generous they can be," she says. "I've found that out in this business."

I put the foam check in the back of the truck and sign the documents she has.

"You should receive the payment in the next couple of days." Amy sticks her hand out, and I shake it.

"Thanks, Amy. And thanks for doing the story on my food truck the other day. It was all you that got this ball rolling."

"You're welcome. I like when a story has a happy ending. Good luck, Kyle."

I watch her sashay off, her cameraman in tow.

The sound of a motorcycle draws my attention, and Rafe backs his bike to the curb.

I sit on the step in the back door, my boots on the pavement. "What are you doing here?"

He climbs off and walks over. "I wanted to talk to you. You got a minute?"

"Yeah." I lift a thumb to the check leaning against the counter. "Channel Five News was just here. Look what they did."

He frowns at the board, and his eyes widen. "What the fuck? They gave you all that money? For real?"

"People saw the story they did the other day about the trouble we had at the festival. The station got a bunch of donations for me. Can you believe that?"

"What are you going to do with it all?"

I rub a hand down my jaw. "I don't know. I haven't had time to think about it."

Rafe lifts a chin to it. "Guess that's enough to start a restaurant, if that's what you still want."

"Yeah, probably." I long to talk about it with Sutton. "Where's Sutton? Why isn't she with you?"

"Your help left town."

"What?" I frown.

"She left this note." He digs a folded piece of paper out of his pocket and hands it to me.

I snatch it and quickly open it, my eyes scanning over the words, a frown deepening my brow.

Rafe,

I hope you and Kyle can work out your rift. Never forget how important family is. You two were the best of brothers, and I hate if I had any part in destroying that.

I think you and I both know this relationship isn't going anywhere serious, so I've left town.

I wish you all the best.

Sutton

My mouth drops open. "So, what are you doing here? Aren't you going after her?"

"Why would I? She's right. I don't have those feelings for her."

I surge to my feet and punch him in the mouth. He staggers backward, and I point a finger at him. "Then you shouldn't have strung her along."

Rafe spits blood on the pavement, then wipes his mouth with the back of his hand. "Fucking hell, Kyle. What was that for?"

"You know what it was for."

He stares at me. "Guess I do. She was right—she did come between us. I should have never cut in on you the day we met her. I knew you liked her. I don't know why I felt like it was a competition, especially when she and I had so little in common. I'm sorry about that, Kyle."

"Well, it's too late now, isn't it?"

"She was right about something else, too."

"What's that?" I ask.

"She was right when she said I've used you."

"She said that?"

"She did. Not sure it was intentional, but I took advantage of you. I'm not sure I realized you felt guilty for what happened to me. I figured you felt sorry for me. And deep down, that pissed me off.

"I guess what I'm trying to say is, I'm sorry for how I acted. Sutton was right. I don't need you to fix things for me. I just need you to be my brother. If she's it for you, you should go for it."

"Go for it?"

"Yeah, go after her. You're the one she wants. Everyone sees it, even me."

"And you don't have a problem with that?"

He grins. "Not saying I won't give you hell, but I want you to be happy, Kyle. If she's the one, then you should be with her."

"For real?"

"You get I don't blame you, right? I had no idea you carried that guilt for what happened to me. Just tell me you know that, brother."

I hold out my hand, and when he takes it, I pull him in for a hug. "I never wanted a woman to come between us, Rafe."

"She won't. You two belong together. You should get her and bring her back."

Rafe's phone goes off, and he answers it. "Hey, Ma. What's up?"

He walks away for a minute, then returns.

"What is it?" I ask. "Is everything all right?"

"She gave Sutton a ride to Diridon Station after the fight, but she doesn't know where she went." Rafe searches my eyes. "She could have caught a train to Stockton or a bus to Santa Cruz."

"Santa Cruz is where we found her. Why would she go to Stockton?"

"She told me once she had a friend there."

"Where?"

He shrugs. "I don't know."

I pull my phone out and try to call her, but it gives me a message that says it's not in service. "Her phone is off."

"How're you gonna find her?" Rafe asks. "We don't even know where to look."

"She must have had family somewhere. What did she tell you?" I press.

"I, uh, I don't know. We never talked about it."

My brows lift. "What do you mean you never talked about it?" I drag a hand through my hair at Rafe's blank look.

"We just didn't have that." He gestures to me. "That easy way of laughing and talking. I mean, I guess we just didn't click. So, no, we didn't talk about shit like that."

"I don't get you, Rafe." I slam the van door, lock up the trailer, and head to the cab of my pickup.

"Where're you goin'?" my brother asks, following me.

"I'm taking the trailer home, then I'm going to find Sutton."

I leave him standing in the road next to my driver's door as I pull from the curb.

CHAPTER TWENTY-THREE

Kyle—

I search Sutton's social media, and message her friends. I make contact with one in Santa Cruz and another in Stockton. Neither have seen her. At least, that's what they tell me. I plead my case, but it falls on deaf ears. When I get nowhere, I ask they pass on a message to please call me, but I don't hold out much hope.

If she doesn't want to be found, her friends aren't going to give her up.

In desperation, I even make a post on the food truck page she started for me. Just four words.

Sutton, please call me.

So far, she hasn't replied, so I do the only other thing I can think to do.

Taking my bike, I ride the hour to Santa Cruz and aimlessly look for her. The wharf is crowded, along with the restaurant where we ate. I stand at the railing for hours, watching people walk past, and all I can think about are all the good times we had together. How she made me laugh, how excited she got helping me with the food truck social media, how we lay on top of Green's RV and watched the stars together, and how I told her about the restaurant I wanted someday, and she told me about the guy blackmailing her.

I long to tell her about Amy Armstrong and the money Channel Five News raised. Sutton was so much a part of everything that occurred to make that happen. If it wasn't for her, I wouldn't have gotten the attention of the food blogger, the Five Forks award, or the invitation to Tribe. If it wasn't for her picture, I'd never have gotten that check. Hell, if it wasn't for Sutton, I probably would have ruined the chicken chili recipe in the first place, and the whole business would have been a failure before it even got off the ground.

But it's more than working together. I look forward to being around her, and that has nothing to do with social media or any awards. It has to do with how happy she makes my day by just being with me.

The sun beats down, and I grab a beer to cool off. I stay until after the sun sets, then ride home once night falls.

As my bike eats up the miles, my mind keeps turning over ideas. I could hire a private detective, or rent a billboard. I could post on her social media every single day. I could do a lot of things, but I can't make her come back to me, if it's not what she wants.

By the time I reach San Jose, the air has turned chilly, and failure sinks into my bones. I have to accept the fact that maybe a relationship wasn't what she wanted after all.

I can't help feeling like I've failed. If only I had done things differently from the start. If only I had pursued her, pushed Rafe aside… she could be with me.

We could be happy.

If only.

Those two words eat at my soul until I want to punch a hole in the wall.

Days pass, and every single one I spend alone, managing the lunch rush, the dinner rush and then doing it all over the next day, working myself into exhaustion so that I fall into bed at night and don't lie awake and stare at the ceiling and think about Sutton.

A week passes, and then a month, and I realize she may never come back.

I pester her friends until they block me.

I spend every free day driving to Santa Cruz and walking the wharf. In my head, I know it makes no sense. It's such a long shot. But in my heart, I feel closer to her here, where we met. And I need to feel close to her.

I watch another sunset, then climb on my bike and ride home.

When I pull in the drive, my mother's car is parked at the curb, and she's sitting on my porch steps.

I'm really not in the mood to talk. I know Mom's been worried about me. She calls me often. But I just want to go to bed.

As I approach, she stands.

"Hey, Ma." I kiss her cheek. "What are you doing here?"

"I want to talk to you."

"You could have just called." I troop up the stairs, exhaustion weighing me down like my boots are made of lead. Unlocking my door, I let her in ahead of me.

"I wanted to see you. You missed family dinner the other night."

Family dinner. Every Tuesday night. I've missed more than one.

"Sorry. I guess it slipped my mind." I toss my keys on the counter. "You want a beer or something?"

"No, thanks. Can we sit?"

I grab a longneck and join her at the table.

"Did you go to Santa Cruz again?" she asks.

I nod.

"No luck?"

"No luck. I don't think I truly expect to find her anymore. But I feel close to her there, and I need that right now."

She reaches across the table and sets her palm on my forearm. "You need something new to focus on."

"I don't feel it, Ma. I have no interest in anything."

"You have to build the life you'd build if she were here. Maybe the universe will bring her to you."

"The universe, huh? Sure, let's try that," I say sarcastically.

"Have you decided what you want to do with that money you received?"

I shake my head. I haven't touched it. I haven't wanted to do anything with it until I could share the news with Sutton, and I stubbornly don't want to give up on that.

"There's a vacant place in San Pedro Square. It's small, but there's a little outdoor patio. I think it would make a wonderful place for your restaurant."

"San Pedro Square? That's got to be a fortune."

"Cole knows the owner of the building. He made a call for you."

"Ma, you shouldn't have asked him to do that."

"I didn't. Your father did."

"Dad? Why?"

"Because he loves you. He got word the guy was looking for a new tenant. The last guy's place went under last month and had to close the doors. Cole got his price down a good bit."

"I don't know."

"It already has a full kitchen. You'd just have to change the signage and paint. Maybe some new tables and chairs. You know, make it your own."

"It's a lot."

"Isn't this what you wanted?"

"Yes. But without Sutton, it all feels meaningless." I scrape my thumb nail down the label of my bottle.

"Baby, look at me."

I lift my eyes.

"You have a family to help you. Hell, you have the entire club to help you. Cole made that phone call for you. He also said they'd help with any labor you need to get it cleaned up and ready. You have to make a life a woman would want to be a part of, son. Make that life."

I stare at her, knowing she's right but finding it hard to find the energy or enthusiasm to do any of it. It sounds exhausting, and I realize I may be in the throes of depression.

She stands and puts her hand on my shoulder, then drops a phone number on the table. "Cole pulled in a favor for you. At least go see the place. Okay?"

She presses a kiss to my forehead. Then walks out the front door.

I follow and stare out the window, making sure she gets in the car safely, and I stay until she drives away.

Then I return to the table and plop down. I stare at the phone number for a long time, before I drag in a long breath and decide to just get it over with. Then I can say I did what she asked.

CHAPTER TWENTY-FOUR

Kyle—

Lifting a taster spoon, I check the big pot of chicken chili, and give Melissa a thumbs up.

"You ready?" I ask.

"Absolutely. Let's kick the tires and take it for a spin, boss."

I chuckle. She's only filling in for the grand opening and until I'm sure my staff is up to the task. "You're adorable. Especially with the apron and hat."

"Hey, this hat beats a hairnet by a mile. And I *am* adorable, thank you very much."

"You talkin' smack, woman?" Billy yells from where he's manning the grill.

"Mind your grill, ol' man," she sasses back.

I check the clock on the wall. "We open in five minutes, people."

"We're ready, boss," Rafe says, sniffling from the chopping block where he's slicing onions.

I look over, his eyes watering.

"You cryin', brother?"

"I'm not crying, you're crying."

I roll my eyes and walk from the kitchen, through the dining room, checking that every table and booth is set up properly with condiments and the specials menus I had printed.

I lift my chin to the prospect in civilian clothes, manning the bar.

"You ready, kid?"

"Ready, boss."

"What's the special today?" I quiz him.

"Two-dollar margaritas and five-dollar pitchers of beer."

"With…?" I drag out the word, reminding him.

"Oh, right. With an entrée purchase."

"What's the limit on the margaritas and pitchers?"

"Two margaritas per person and two pitchers per table."

I give him a thumbs up. "Make sure the servers get the food orders. I'm not giving away booze for nothing. I want repeat food customers."

"Got it. No food, no special."

At the door, Brandy is set up at the hostess podium, prepared to seat people, a stack of menus at the ready. I give her a hug.

"Thanks for doing this on your day off, hon."

"I'm glad to help, Kyle. And if the prospect needs help, I'm an experienced bartender."

"Gonna quit your day job?"

She bites her lip. "Maybe I can fill in on weekends."

"Let's hope the place takes off first."

"Oh, it will. I'm sure of it. Especially with the University so close."

I walk to the door and step outside. My entire club is out there dressed in street clothes, making it look like we've already got a crowd waiting.

I spot my president and walk over and give him a back-slapping hug. "Thanks for everything, Prez. You're a big part of making this happen."

Cole grins. "I believe in you, Kyle. You've always had that go-get-'em work ethic. I know you'll bust your ass to make this a success."

"Gonna try."

"In the meantime, you can park the food truck at the clubhouse."

"Thanks. I appreciate that."

"And maybe do a Sunday barbeque for us now and then."

"I knew there had to be a catch," I reply with a chuckle.

"There always is, brother."

My mother rushes over. "I want to get a group shot. Everyone, bunch together."

We all put our arms around each other and my father points up at the sign.

She gets a good shot and I give her a hug. "Thanks, Ma." Then I turn to the crowd. "Come on in, everyone. We're officially open!"

There's a round of applause, and everyone files in. There are even several actual customers mingled in. My crew knows to take care of them first.

Green stands on the sidewalk with flyers, waving people in. He winks at me, then continues on like a carnival barker.

"Come on in, folks. Best food on the block. Try the homemade onion rings. You'll see I'm not lyin'. Two-dollar margaritas. Five-dollar pitchers. You can't beat that with a stick, mister."

I chuckle and walk inside.

Soon the place is bustling with business.

We're about two hours in when Brandy calls me to the front door.

"Yeah, sweetheart. What do you need?" I see there aren't any customers at her podium.

"There's a woman outside who wants to talk to you. She gave me this." Brandy hands me a folder. For a split second, my heart races and my hope soars that it may be Sutton out there. But she wouldn't be leaving a folder. I flip it open. Inside is a Five Forks Award Winner certificate and a yellow sticky note that reads, *Suitable for framing. I expect to see this up on the wall in a prominent position ~ Food Truck Tina.*

"She's waiting outside?" I ask.

"Yes."

I step through the door and see her. She greets me with a smile, and I extend my hand.

"Tina? I'm Kyle. I finally get to meet you face-to-face." I hold up the folder. "You changed my life with this, you know?"

She grins. "I'm so happy to see all your success. It really does my heart good. I saw on your social media page you were opening a brick and mortar, and I had to see the place for myself. I've been meaning to interview you. Maybe you've got a minute for that?" She holds up her phone.

"For you, anything. In fact, come inside. Lunch is on the house."

"First this," she says, and turns on her phone and gets the two of us in the shot.

"I'm here today in San Jose with Kyle. Most of you may remember him as our latest Five Forks Award winner. Well, I'm happy to say Kyle has found a permanent home here in San Jose at San Pedro Square on the corner of West Santa Clara. But *Kyle's* isn't quite accurate anymore, is it?"

Then she points to the sign on the brick wall.

I stare at the new signage. "No, I suppose not."

"Why'd you change the name?"

"I named it after my lost love—the woman I foolishly let get away."

She gets a shot of the sign, then looks at the camera. "You heard it here, folks. The inside scoop. *Sutton's Place* is named after his lost love. Sutton, honey, if you're out there, you're letting a good one get away." Then she leans to the camera and whispers, "Don't be a fool."

She pulls back. "So, Kyle, what's on the menu today?"

I tell her our menu and specials, and once again she leans to the camera.

"Did you hear that, peeps? Two-dollar margaritas! I'm in

heaven!"

She's funny and bubbly, and I love her immediately.

"Come on in, darlin'. I'll set you up right."

She looks at the camera and fans her face. "He called me darlin'. And he's got a beard and tattoos. Ladies, take my advice, and make a beeline down here."

CHAPTER TWENTY-FIVE

Kyle—

Sunday after closing, I invite my brothers to the restaurant to help me celebrate. We push a bunch of tables together to form one long one.

One prospect scurries around the table, passing out shot glasses to everyone, and another prospect follows behind with a bottle of whiskey.

I stand at the head and lift my shot in the air. "I want to thank each and every one of you for pitching in and making this place a success. Thanks to all of you, it only took six weeks to get the place open. And you all made opening day a huge success. We've had a hell of a first week. I couldn't have done it without you. Truly."

"Yeah, even though Green scared away more people than he wrangled in," Shane ribs.

"Hey, I did a bang-up job, shithead. You want to stand out on the street and sweet talk the girls? Go ahead. Maybe take your shirt off while you're at it."

"Brothers. Everyone contributed." I focus in on Shane. "And you can have a shift next Saturday."

"What?" he barks.

"Shirtless," Cole decrees. "That's an order."

"Goddamn it. So, I'm just a piece of meat?"

"Yes!" they all roar in unison.

Green laughs and points. "I'm gonna film the whole thing, pretty boy. You better brush off your dance moves."

"Dance moves?"

"You don't think you can just stand out there, do ya?" Green snaps. "You gotta dance around like them pizza boys do. I'll get you a sign you can spin."

Cole shakes with laughter. "You were saying, Kyle?"

"I especially want to thank you, Prez. If you hadn't worked your magic and got the landlord down on the price, I never could have afforded this place."

He grins. "It wasn't so much magic as arm-twisting, kid."

"I stand corrected." I lift my glass. "Thank you."

He clinks his glass to mine. "To Kyle. You worked your butt off, and we're all proud of you."

At that, my father stands. "I'd like to make a toast, if I could, son."

I nod. "Sure, Dad."

"Floor's yours, Wolf," Cole says, taking a seat.

"First off, you and Rafe had some rough spots lately, but you worked through them, and now you're both back to the way you were before. I couldn't be prouder of the two of you. And Kyle, you had a dream, and you worked hard to make it happen. A man can't do more than that in this life. You found something you love, and you get to do it. When you enjoy your work, it's not work, it's fun. So, here's hoping you have a lot of fun running this place."

"Here, here," the crowd says, downing their shots.

Wolf walks over and hugs me, slapping my back.

"Thanks, Dad."

There's a tap on the front glass door.

Crystal jumps to her feet. "That'll be the bakery. I ordered a cake."

"A cake?" I protest, but she's already up to answer it.

I pick up the bottle of whiskey. "Who wants another?"

"You gotta ask?" Red Dog replies.

"Everyone, kid," Crash barks. "Hop to it."

"How about some bowls of that chicken chili?" Green asks. "You're feeding us, right?"

I laugh and glance up to see my mother walking toward me with a funny look on her face. Then she steps aside, and Sutton is standing behind her, a bouquet of flowers in her hand.

The room suddenly gets silent.

"Sutton?" I whisper.

She doesn't look anywhere but at me, and it's like we're the only two people in the room.

"Congratulations on your place, Kyle. Really. It's fantastic."

I swallow. "How did you know?"

"I saw Tina's post."

"Ah. I see." I nod to the flowers. "You just stopped by to congratulate me, then?"

Her eyes stray to the long table filled with my brothers and their ol' ladies. "Well, I wanted to talk to you…"

My father folds his arms. "Anything you got to say, you can say in front of all of us."

Her gaze shifts briefly to Rafe, then back to me. "I wanted to tell you… you see, I wanted to ask…"

I wait, my chest squeezed into a tight band. I'm afraid to hope.

"Spit it out, girl," Green says.

"Green, hush," my mother snaps.

"I guess what I'm trying to say is… I've been miserable without you, and I'd like to give us a chance." She looks down at the flowers, then holds them out. "Will you go out with me, Kyle?"

I grin and run to her, lifting her off her feet and twirling her around. Her arms wrap my neck, and she buries her face in my shoulder. When I set her on her feet, I hear my MC brothers' wisecracks.

"Guess that's your answer, girl," Green says.

"I think that's a yes," Red Dog says with a laugh.

"How come you never asked me out on a date?" Reckless says to Harley Jean, who smacks him on the arm.

No matter the conversations around us, my focus is intently on Sutton. I cup her face and pull her mouth to mine for our first kiss. Having it in front of the entire club was not the dream I had in my head, but I'll take it. I'll take her... any way I can get her.

Her lips are soft, and the kiss is sweet and innocent, with the promise of so much more. More that I want to explore and partake of, the sooner the better.

When I break away, I look at the table full of people. "Party's over. Everybody out."

Cole raises a brow at me, daring to give him an order, but he grins and stands. "You heard the man. Out."

Green scrapes his chair across the floor. "We didn't even get chili."

Sara puts her hand over his mouth. "Hush. You can take me out to dinner."

"I thought that's what I was doin' here."

She pushes him toward the door. "Go."

My mother cups Sutton's face, staring into her eyes with a smile. "I'm so glad you came home." Then she hugs her, breaks off and hugs me, then leads my father out with the others.

"Give me a second," I say, kissing Sutton's hand and moving to the door to lock up after everyone files out.

Sutton sets the flowers on the table, and I grin as I walk back to her. "No one's ever brought me flowers before."

"Well, I felt like I messed up when I left town, so I needed to go all-out."

I take her hands in mine. "What made you come back?"

"Besides the fact that I missed you terribly?" She looks around the place. "You named it after me."

"I did."

"Why?"

"I hoped for this. That you'd see it and come back to me."

Her eyes glaze. "I'm sorry I left."

"You're here now." I brush a tear away with my thumb. "That's all that matters." Then I grin. "You want to see the place?"

"Yes, but Kyle, how did you afford all this? You lost all that money."

"That's the best part. God, I've been dying to share this with you. You'll never guess what happened. Not in a million years." I loop my arm around her shoulders, walk her into the kitchen, and tell her all about it.

We end up getting two bowls of chili and eating our first meal together in our restaurant. And it is *our* restaurant. That's how I've always thought of it.

I find a candle and light it.

"I want you to be a part of this. It's your dream too, right? A family business?" I kiss her hand, and she nods. "I wanted this for both of us."

"It was stupid of me to leave."

"I understood why you did it, but God, it killed me. I wish you'd answered my calls. I tried everything I could think of to get in touch with you. Did your girlfriends tell you that?"

She nods. "I wasn't sure I could see a way for us to be together without it destroying your relationship with Rafe."

"We had a long talk. He's fine with it. He told me you were right, that the two of you just didn't have what you and I have. He wants me to be happy."

"I'm so glad. I've been sick about it."

I hold her hand and rub my thumb absently across hers. "It's been hell these last couple of months. I rode to Santa Cruz I don't know how many times."

"You did?"

"I'd stand on the wharf and search the crowd, hoping somehow I'd find you. It was the only place I knew to go. I guess it sounds idiotic, huh?"

She shakes her head, her eyes filling. "It sounds like a man in love."

"I am in love, Sutton. I love you." I blow out a breath. "Wow. I said it."

She squeezes my hand. "I love you, too, Kyle. All the time we spent together, every day I felt it growing stronger until I didn't know what to do with it. I had all these feelings for you, but I couldn't express them. I wasn't supposed to be feeling them."

I tug her off her chair and into my lap. "That's over now. We don't have to hold back anymore." I rub my hand up her hip. "I've wanted to touch you for so long."

She strokes my face and cups my jaw. "Me, too." She presses her lips to mine. And this kiss is much more than the last one.

There are no prying eyes, and I pull her closer. My tongue chases hers.

Finally, we break apart. I want so much more, but I don't want to rush her.

I press my forehead to hers. "I want to take you out on a date. Someplace nice. Where ever you want. You choose."

"Kyle?"

"Yeah, babe?"

"Right now, I want you to take me home with you."

I search her eyes. "You mean that, Sutton?"

She nods. "I can't wait to be with you, to have you hold me, kiss me, make love to me."

My dick is already hard, but her words send another wave of blood south. "Let's get out of here, then."

CHAPTER TWENTY-SIX

Sutton—

Kyle and I make out at every stoplight between the restaurant and his house. When we pull into the driveway, he tugs my hand, and we dash up the porch steps. Once we're through the doorway, he spins me around and kisses me, pushing me against the wall. He goes at me like a starving man.

Before I know what he's about to do, he puts a shoulder to my belly and hefts me up. I shriek. "Kyle, what are you doing? Put me down."

Ignoring me, he carries me through the house and drops me to my back on his big bed. I bounce once, and his deliciously hard body comes down on me.

Leaning over, his thumb strokes my cheeks gently, and his gaze locks with mine.

"Seems I've wanted you since the moment I laid eyes on you."

"And now you have me."

"Those months you were gone… God, how I missed you."

"I missed you, too, Kyle. So much."

"You have no idea how long I've wanted this, how often I'd come home after spending all day working beside you only to lie in this bed and think about what it would be like to make love to you."

"Tell me."

"I imagined what it would feel like to run my hands over your soft skin, to thread my fingers in your glossy curls, and to sink my dick into your sweet, wet pussy, feeling it tighten around me."

"I dreamed of you, too. I ached to have you touch me, to have your body pressed to mine like this. I thought I'd never know."

"I'm here now, baby."

His mouth descends over mine, kissing me ravenously, demandingly. It makes my head spin.

His beard brushes against my skin, and I moan, wanting it to brush over every inch of my body—my throat, my breasts, my belly, my thighs. Anticipation grabs hold of me, and my hands slide into his hair, pulling him closer and urging him on. His body responds, his muscles tightening and his hips arching.

He drags his mouth to my ear.

"I never should have let you go. I should have stopped you. I should have told Rafe I wanted you. We've wasted so much time. But I'm gonna make up for it. I'm gonna make it all up to you, Sutton. I swear."

My legs lock around him. "I love you."

His beautiful mouth descends to mine again. This time his kiss is more urgent, filled with all the pent-up desire we both feel. Desperate, needy, ravenous.

He tugs my shirt over my head with a whoosh, then yanks me to the edge of the bed. His hot gaze drifts over my neck, my collarbone, to the rounded cleavage pushing from my bra.

His chin lifts. "Take it off."

I reach behind me, unhook it, and toss it aside.

His hungry eyes take me in, moving over every inch of me. It's the first time he's seen me, and it's erotic as hell.

He drops to his knees, dips his head, and his mouth latches onto one nipple, his strong arms banding around my ribs.

My head falls back, and I thrust my chest up for his greedy lips, letting my hands glide gently over his biceps and shoulders to his neck.

I hold him against me, loving the feel of his mouth on my nipples—licking, sucking, teasing, tormenting until I'm desperate for more.

"Kyle…" I moan.

He reads me like a book and sucks hard, sending a jolt straight to my pussy. A gasp escapes me.

He moves to the other nipple. Another hard tug of his mouth sends a second jolt through me. I grab one of his hands and bring it to the fastening of my jeans. He gets the message and breaks off to yank them down my legs, tossing them on the floor.

Then he stands and strips, tearing his shirt over his head, tossing it aside, and then those big hands work the buckle of his belt.

I shudder in a breath at the erotic sight. His eyes never leave mine. But mine take it all in—his chest, his abs, the muscles in his arms flexing as he works the belt free.

Finally, his cock springs forth into his palm, and he gives it a stroke from root to tip, twisting the head.

I wet my lips and a rush of desire wets my pussy. God, I want him so badly.

He crawls over me, pushing me to the mattress, one hand planted in the bed, one warm palm settling low on my soft belly. The heat of his touch sinks into my skin, and that's all it takes to make me his. Completely.

His gaze bores into me. He hesitates, drawing the moment out, and my chest rises and falls in anticipation. My tongue slips out to wet my lips, and his eyes drop to them. He lowers his head until his mouth brushes mine. My palms move up his chest, gliding over his skin, and he trembles and whispers against my lips.

"I prayed to God he'd bring you back to me, and He did. I promised Him I'd be the man you deserved."

"You are. You're everything I need."

"I want to take my time. I don't want to rush this."

His hand travels slowly up my thigh, and his eyes follow it, drifting nearer to my waiting pussy.

"You're the prettiest thing I've ever seen, sweetheart."

My hips lift, urgently wanting his touch. "Please, baby."

He puts a hand to each knee, spreading me open. "I want to taste you. Lie back."

I do as he asks, my belly quivering.

His mouth covers me, softly at first, teasing, gentle licks designed to arouse and torment until I'm undulating beneath him. My hips lift, following his mouth, desperate for more. When I can't take it anymore, he doesn't deny me. He slips two fingers inside while his thumb begins its own stroking rhythm. Over and over and over and over. He won't let up until I'm thrashing on the bed, my hips meeting each stroke, each glorious sensation.

"Kyle…" I pant.

"My baby's so damn wet for me. Goddamn, I want you. I want to sink my dick inside your sweet pussy." His voice is like a drug, sucking me under.

His words bring me even closer to orgasm. "Please," I beg, in a whisper. "*Please.*"

His mouth comes down on me, and my head arches back. I suck in a shuddering breath and hold it. I soar higher until I'm teetering on the edge, and the fingers of his other hand pinch hard on my nipple. I tumble over the edge in an explosive orgasm that has me groaning out loud.

My arousal coats his hand as I gasp for breath and float down to earth. Kyle withdraws his fingers and licks them clean, then soothes my pussy lips with soft nuzzles.

He doesn't let up until I'm aroused all over again. "That's my girl," he urges me on.

I clutch at him, trying to pull him up to me. "Kyle, please. I need you inside me."

"I thought you'd never ask." He slides over my body and surges inside me with one forceful thrust, sinking all the way.

I gasp at his entry.

"You're mine, now," he whispers.

"Yes," I respond.

"Forever," he adds.

"Forever." I brush my thumb over his lower lip. He begins to move inside me, gliding in and out, each stroke becoming more urgent. He stares at me, our eyes locked as his chest grows slick and his hair dampens. His breathing labors, and his pulse pounds in a vein in his throat.

I tighten my legs around him, my pussy clamping down on him, and he thrusts one final time, roaring out his climax, then collapsing on top of me.

I love the feel of his weight. My mouth moves to his throat, pressing soft, loving kisses from his collarbone, to his jaw, to his ear. I nuzzle and nip at his earlobe.

He groans, and the vibration rumbles through his chest. My hands slide along his spine, to the dimples at the base, to his butt cheeks."

I feel so satisfied, so happy, so truly content for the first time in so long. I feel like we've built a bridge to each other—one that is strong enough to last a lifetime.

Still buried inside me, he lifts enough to take my face in his hands.

"Ma told me I need to be the man who deserved you."

"You are. Absolutely."

"I swear I'll be the best man I can be for you and for our children some day."

I nod, my eyes filling.

"Are those happy tears?" he asks.

"Yes. Very happy tears. I don't need anything but your love."

"You have it, pretty girl. All of it." He presses a soft kiss to my mouth. "I do love you, baby. So very much."

"I love you, too."

He pulls out and falls to the bed beside me, taking me in his arms.

I tuck my head under his chin, my cheek to his chest, and listen to his heartbeat.

His fingers coast up and down my spine, and I idly drag a fingertip over the lines of his tattoos.

"How do you like what I did with the restaurant?" he asks.

"I love it."

"Any suggestions? Anything we should do differently?"

I smile, loving that Kyle seems to like cuddling and talking in hushed voices. I love to listen to his deep voice, and soon, it lulls me to sleep.

CHAPTER TWENTY-SEVEN

Kyle—

We spend Sunday and Monday in bed together, barely coming up for air to get food.

It's mid-morning on Tuesday, and Sutton is still asleep when I slip from the bed and tug on my jeans. Padding into the kitchen, I start a pot of coffee, then go out to the deck to touch base with TJ.

ME: YOU UP?

TJ: YEAH, LOVER BOY. YOU COME UP FOR AIR? WE'VE GOT CHURCH TONIGHT.

ME: NICE OF PREZ TO CUT ME ONE DAY SLACK.

TJ: YOU KNOW MY OL' MAN.

ME: I'VE GOT A FAVOR TO ASK

TJ: DON'T YOU ALWAYS

ME: I NEED YOU TO GET A VEST THAT'LL FIT SUTTON AND A PROPERTY PATCH TO GO WITH IT.

TJ: WOW. THAT WAS FAST.

ME: WHEN YOU KNOW, YOU KNOW

TJ: YOU SURE ABOUT THIS, BRO? THAT'S A BIG STEP. HUGE.

ME: WERE YOU SURE ABOUT GIGI?

TJ: TOUCHE

ME: WE'VE SPENT A LOT OF TIME TOGETHER. WE'VE TALKED ABOUT WHAT WE WANT OUR FUTURE TO BE. I KNOW HER LIKE I'VE NEVER REALLY KNOWN A WOMAN BEFORE. SHE'S THE ONE, TJ. I FEEL IT IN MY BONES.

TJ: I'M HAPPY FOR YOU, KYLE. REALLY HAPPY.

ME: THANKS

TJ: I'LL TAKE CARE OF IT. WHEN YOU GONNA DO IT?

ME: AFTER CHURCH TONIGHT IF YOU CAN GET IT DONE.

TJ: YOU DON'T ASK FOR MUCH, DO YA?

ME: SORRY

TJ: I'LL DO MY BEST. WE'VE GOT THAT LADY WHO MAKES ALL OUR PATCHES. I'LL TELL HER IT'S FOR A LOVE SICK FOOL.

ME: TELL HER WHATEVER YOU NEED TO GET THE JOB DONE. TELL HER THERE'S A HUNDRED BUCKS IN IT FOR HER IF SHE FINISHES IT BY SUNSET.

TJ: ANYTHING ELSE, TASKMASTER?

ME: THINK YOU CAN MAKE SURE ALL THE OL' LADIES ARE PRESENT TONIGHT?

TJ: SHOULDN'T BE TOO HARD. YOU WANT ME TO CALL YOUR MA?

ME: NO. I'LL DO THAT

TJ: HAVE YOU TALKED TO RAFE YET?

ME: I'M GONNA TAKE A RIDE OVER TO HIS

PLACE IN A BIT.

TJ: OKAY. SEE YOU TONIGHT.

I shove my phone in my hip pocket and grab a cup of coffee. When I carry it in the bedroom, Sutton's eyes pop open.

"I wondered where you'd gone," she murmurs.

Setting the mug down, I plant two fists on the mattress and lean to kiss her gently on the mouth. "Mornin', babe."

"Good morning." She stretches like a cat—a well-satisfied cat.

"You sleep well?"

"I slept great." Her stomach rumbles.

"Sounds like I need to feed my woman."

"I am starved."

She scoots against the headboard, and I pass her the steaming mug. She breathes in the aroma and moans around a sip.

Then I set the mug on the nightstand and slowly tug the sheet until those pretty tits come into view. I dip my head and suck first one, and then the other, until she's moaning and writhing.

When I pull back, I grin. "I'll start breakfast, but first… this."

Quick as lightning, I scoop her up and over my shoulder. She shrieks as I carry her to the bathroom. Setting her down, I turn on the shower and adjust the temperature. Then I drop my jeans to the floor, and my long, hard cock springs forward, bobbing against my abs.

Her tongue darts out to wet her lips, and I feel a rush of arousal.

My eyes hood in desire, and I pull her with me under the spray. Both our bodies are soon slick with rivulets of steamy water trailing over our skin. I hike her in my arms, pin her against the wall, and spread her legs wide.

Grasping my cock in one fist, I swirl the wide head through her wetness, brushing in circles around her sensitive clit.

She moans.

I rotate the head over and over, growling with desire, then dip the crown between her pussy lips, dragging it up and down until she bucks against it.

"Show me how much you want my dick, beautiful."

She rolls her hips and splays her legs wider. I move then, putting my dick to her slick entrance. My strong arms hold her with her back pressed to the tile wall.

Her legs clamp around my waist, and I thrust into her tight, wet pussy.

I hook my arms under her knees, pinning her wide open for me. Dipping my head to watch, I slowly draw my thick cock out until just the head remains.

"You want my dick, baby girl? Your tight little pussy was made for it, wasn't it?"

"Yes," she groans, whimpering. "Please."

"You've had my cock hard for you since the moment I first laid eyes on you." I set a slow rhythm, gently fucking her. "You can't imagine the number of times I jerked off to the thought of you. Stood in this fucking shower with my dick in my hand and imagined your mouth sucking me off."

She wriggles, but she can't move; I've got her pinned.

I thrust faster until her gorgeous breasts are bouncing. "Can you feel me?"

"Yes."

"How far?"

"So deep."

I move one hand, take my thumb, and rub her clit. "Come all over me, angel."

Her body reacts to my words. I watch waves of pleasure cross her lidded gaze.

Finally, I grab her hips, and my orgasm explodes through me.

When I shudder out every last drop, my hold on her loosens until she's on her feet. I press my forehead to her shoulder, my breath sawing in and out. Then I drag my lips and tongue along her collarbone and up her neck until I'm nibbling on her ear. "You are mine, Sutton. Right?"

"Yes."

"Tell me you've always been mine," I demand, needing the words.

"It's always been you, Kyle. Always."

I kiss her deeply, then pull back, grinning. "Now you can have breakfast."

EPILOGUE

Kyle—

Arriving at the clubhouse as darkness falls, I note all the changes in my life. I remember not too long ago, a time when I sat at the bar and watched my brother walk into this clubhouse with Sutton holding his hand.

Now it's my bike she climbs off. My hand she holds. Me she walks in with. None of this escapes me. Nor does the fact of how lucky I am.

She walked into my life like a ray of sunshine. I let her slip through my fingers the first time. But I won't ever let that happen again.

I tug her to my side and enter.

My brothers all turn, and Green starts clapping. "Look who came up for air. Nice of you to let her breathe, Kyle."

I grin, but I don't mind his ribbing. I'm too happy to complain.

"Can we get this damn meeting started now?" Cole growls, tossing back his drink and rising from his barstool.

Cupping Sutton's neck, I press a kiss to her lips. "This shouldn't take too long. Go wait with the other girls at the bar."

She turns, and Melissa motions her over. "Come sit with us, Sutton."

I follow my brothers down the hall, taking my place against the wall while the officers take the chairs.

Cole dispenses with the formalities, calling the meeting to order and going over some business. Apparently, Rafe hasn't paid his dues.

He spreads his hands. "I'll be a little late, but I'll get it."

Cole leans on his elbows. "I called this meeting because of Joselyn Silver."

That perks up everyone in the room.

"I thought that got taken care of," Shane asks.

Prez shakes his head. "She won't quit. Daytona says she's been to Vegas twice now."

"Good thing we put that tracker on her Mercedes," Crash mutters, dragging a hand down his face.

Red Dog leans forward. "There's no way she can get to these guys, is there? I mean, from what Trick said, *he* couldn't get near them."

"You gave her the money back." TJ reminds his father.

"I did."

"So, how's it our problem?" Wolf asks.

"I'd like to prevent her from ending up face down in a reservoir," Cole snaps.

My father lifts his palms in the air. "Fine. You got any ideas?"

"Maybe the FBI needs to have a chat with her," Crash says, steepling his hands.

"The FBI?" Cole asks, leaning in his chair. "You got some personal connections I don't know about, VP?"

Crash grins. "Maybe they're not actual FBI. Maybe they just *look* like FBI. We could probably fool her."

Cole laughs and lifts a hand around the room. "And which of these bearded, tattooed badasses you figure for that clean-cut job, dumbass?"

"I'm sure we could find someone to play the part."

"Yeah, who?"

"Doesn't the councilman owe you a favor?"

Cole stokes his chin, and we can all see the wheels turning. His chair creaks as he leans forward and points a finger at Crash. "You might have something there, VP."

The meeting drones on for another half hour as they toss ideas back and forth and make a plan, but all I can think about is Sutton.

TJ is standing next to me, and I catch his eye and mouth the words, "You get it?"

He nods.

Cole notices. "You boys got something you want to share with the class?"

He makes us feel like fourth grades getting caught passing notes.

TJ throws me under the bus. "Kyle is just impatient to get on to the next of the evening's festivities."

Cole's eyes shift to me. "That so?"

Green is tipped back in his chair, but brings the front legs down with a bang. "Oh, that's right. Word is he's got a property patch to hand out. Sweet love is in the air."

Cole rolls his eyes and slams the gavel down. "Fine. Meeting adjourned."

We trudge out the door, and Green throws his arm around me. "Now there's a way to do this thing, kid."

"Do it any way you want," Red Dog disagrees. "Leave him alone, Green."

"Hey, I'm practically his cupid. I set him up with the Love Machine, didn't I? I think I oughta get some credit for makin' this whole thing happen."

"You get no credit," my father snaps.

"Yeah, what Wolf said," Shane mutters, shoving Green's head.

We walk out into the main room, and the ladies spin around.

Cole drags a chair out into the center and crooks a finger at Sutton. "Come here, girlie."

She looks like a deer in the headlights but does as he says.

"It's all you, kid," Cole says, slapping my shoulder.

A moment later, TJ walks over with the vest.

I take it and turn to face the love of my life.

"Sutton, I'm asking you to wear this. It means you're mine. Always. Forever. No more running away. Understand?"

"That's romantic, brother," Rafe says, sarcasm biting his tone.

I give him a death glare, and he lifts his palms up, laughing. Turning to Sutton, I hold the vest up, letting her read it. "I want you to be my ol' lady, Sutton. You gotta tell me now—yes or no. You know I love you, and I'll do anything for you, girl. So how 'bout it?"

"Say yes, Sutton!" the girls all scream.

She stands. "Yes, baby. I want to be your ol' lady. More than anything."

I swoop her into my arms and twirl her around.

"Good thing you said yes, Sutton," TJ adds. "He had to pay a hundred bucks extra to get the patch lady to make that for you in a rush job."

I set her down and slip it on her, then bend her back with a big kiss, and all my brothers and their ol' ladies cheer.

I know in my heart Sutton and I have a bright future. With her by my side, there's nothing we can't do.

I hope you enjoyed KYLE: Sins of the Father (Book Six)
Read on for a preview of the next installment in the series, RAFE.

RAFE: Sins of the Father
Evil Dead MC – Second Generation

The bad boy and the good girl.

I just started a new job at a lumber mill in the mountains outside of town.

It's just a job to me, until I lay eyes on the owner's daughter.

Then everything changes.

I need this job, and she's the definition of off-limits—the boss's daughter.

I should stay away. I know better than to mess with a good girl like her.

The first time she notices me, I'm being handcuffed and put in the back of a squad car.

Fantastic.

After that, she turns her nose up at me, like I'm trash.

Our mutual disdain builds and keeps a needed wall between us.

She stays up the hill at the big house with the wrap-around porch, and I stay down by the mill.

Until one night, tragedy strikes, and I'm the only one left working, the only one there to protect her and take care of her.

All of a sudden, our differences aren't so sharp, and our mutual disdain melts away as we finally see each other more deeply.

A friendship builds, and soon turns to *a secret love that burns hot in the dark of night.*

Preorder RAFE now

For a list of all my books, please visit my website.
Evil Dead MC series
Brothers Ink Tattoo series
Devil Kings MC series
Soul Sisters Duet
FRENCH QUARTER CHRISTMAS: An Evil Dead MC Holiday
Romance
Tri Star Security series
Kings of Carnage MC series: SLY and SAINT
Royal Bastards MC Series
Sins of the Father: Evil Dead MC – Second Generation series
Saints Outlaws MC series

Made in the USA
Monee, IL
02 January 2025

75780351R00121